A VERY BIG BANG

A 'SIMON SHARD' NOVEL

Philip McCutchan

A Lythway Book

CHIVERS PRESS
BATH

First published in Great Britain 1975
by
Hodder & Stoughton Limited
This Large Print edition published by
Chivers Press
by arrangement with
the author
1992

ISBN 0 7451 1586 1

British Library Cataloguing in Publication Data available

Photoset, printed and bound in Great Britain by
REDWOOD PRESS LIMITED, Melksham, Wiltshire

A VERY BIG BANG

A VERY BIG BANG

Casey had an assignation in York with a very beautiful woman. And that was his undoing. All he could tell the Security Service was that there would be four men to carry the explosives. So it was going to be a very big bang, and it would happen within ten days somewhere in the London Underground system. But Casey never made it to his debriefing with Detective Chief Superintendent Simon Shard. Shard had to pick up the slender clues himself. And he had to do it before a lethal device brought about the point of no return for London's commuting millions.

CHAPTER ONE

The curiously shaped bundle, as dawn began to lighten the water between Westminster and Waterloo bridges, sogged just below the scummy surface of the river, sometimes up a little, and visible, as it twisted in the current; sometimes down, and visible only from directly above by the sharp-eyed gulls that wheeled in search of garbage. From time to time there was a thin trail of blood to be seen, had anyone been looking, blood that dribbled from the stained sacking that held the body. There was no attempt at concealment, no weighting to carry the sack's contents down to hug the bottom of the river: it floated free, making down on the ebb-tide towards Greenwich, Tilbury, Gravesend, the open sea. That, at least, would have been its inevitable direction until it was in due course turned back on its tracks by the flood-tide. In the event, it neither reached the sea nor was tide-turned: it beached. A quirk of the Thames took charge. After passing beneath Waterloo Bridge, along below the Embankment, past the Temple with other of the Inns of Court beyond the Strand, under Blackfriars Bridge and on towards Tower Bridge, past ancient dungeons and keeps, it passed into the area of old, derelict wharves and warehouses. Here were the ghosts of trading empires that had emptied and filled the holds of ships from all the world's ports, linking the London river to Cathay and the Orient, to South America and Australasia in a grand, vast sweep of enterprise. It was here amid the wreck of past glories, on the Wapping side, that the sack and its grisly contents beached, to be left high and dry as the ebb lowered the water-level still further. It lay bloodily on a small segment of stony, muddy ground, cold, forlorn, very still and silent.

★   ★   ★

The day before, Shard, in his office in Seddon's Way, had carried out a simple act: he had answered his telephone. Yet he decided afterwards that it had been just one of those odd things: when the phone had buzzed, he'd happened, just happened, to be thinking about London's underground—maybe because, till the phone had called him, he had been about to go home on the network. A tube was a tube was a tube, world without end except during strikes, and that was all it meant to London's commuting millions—until something went wrong, anyhow.

The phone: it sounded urgent. Shard had a sixth sense about his telephone. He crossed his office, two strides from the dirty window for long legs.

'Shard.'

'It's Casey, Mr Shard.'

'Hold.' Slewing, Shard reached for a pad of paper and a biro. Casey came on the line, broad Dublin, and Shard spoke with the handset jammed into his collar. 'Go ahead, Tom, I'm listening.'

'Are you now.' The voice sounded thin, a little out of breath, and, faintly, scared. 'Then hold onto your hat, Mr Shard.' There was a pause: Shard heard the flick of a lighter, followed by a deep suck and a long blow. His nerves rasped at him but he held back on his impatience: Casey couldn't do anything without a fag in his mouth, which held certain dangers for an explosives expert. Casey went on: 'I have the date, positive.'

'Well?'

'May fourth.'

Shard said, 'Ten days ... fair warning. Well done! Where?'

There was a curious, almost virgin surprise in Casey's voice as though he still couldn't believe it. 'The underground,' he said. 'London underground—'

'A station?'

'Not a station. A section of track ... this is big, Mr Shard, the biggest yet. Four men, no less, to carry the explosives.' There was a pause. 'Look, Mr Shard. I've a lot to tell. I

3

think we should meet.'

Shard thought fast: meetings could be dangerous but Casey was experienced enough to know that and to balance the risks involved. Looking at his watch Shard asked, 'Where are you—here in London?'

'Yes. I left York mid-afternoon.'

'Uh-huh. How was York, Tom?'

'The daffodils,' Casey said nostalgically, 'were lovely.' Casey was a frustrated countryman at heart, never mind a lifetime in the Dublin CID. 'Where do we meet, Mr Shard, and when?'

'Berserk Strip Club, Soho,' Shard said, 'at 8.30. Okay?'

'Okay,' Casey answered, and rang off. Shard frowned, then took up his security line, calling the switchboard over in the Foreign Office. 'Chief Superintendent Shard. I'd like you to call my wife. I'll be late home. Tell her I'm sorry.'

'Very good, sir.'

Shard put down the handset, frowning still, conscious of his cowardice. He hated hearing the disappointment in Beth's voice. It was getting altogether too frequent that something had to be put off at the last moment: tonight it was to have been dinner in Chelsea. Shard gave a heavy sigh: one of the nicer things he'd hoped for when he'd allowed himself to be persuaded into leaving the Special Branch on secondment to Hedge's box of funny tricks at the Foreign

4

Office, was more time for Beth; but it hadn't worked out that way at all.

*   *   *

Earlier that same day, in York, Detective Sergeant Casey from Dublin had for the first time met the person he had thought of as Mr Big, only this person had turned out to be Miss Big. And she had fascinated Casey—who for current purposes was not Casey but Timothy O'Phelan from Clonmel in County Tipperary. Miss Big was just a slip of a girl in Casey's eyes, barely skimming twenty. The face was striking: olive-skinned, with a bold nose and straight, dark eyebrows. The eyes themselves were dark but brilliant, and as hard as black diamonds: not exactly a pretty face—there was too much character and too much passionate dedication for mere prettiness to be appropriate—but strongly sexual even if currently the passion was not for matters of the body. The brows curved down, forming a T-junction with the nose; the hair, black as the eyes, lay close along the cheeks, curling up beneath the strong chin, its ends played with by slim, olive fingers. The lips—soft, moist, very red and full—were made for kissing, for the things of life, yet they spoke of death.

Listening to the girl that morning were three men, plus Casey: three of an indeterminate

Middle Eastern origin, as was the girl herself. Casey studied them while he memorised the instructions that came from those rose-red lips. Into his consciousness came other sounds also, distantly, through the open window: the clack and clatter of inter-city trains from north and south, the small collisions of shunted rolling stock in the marshalling yard, sounds of peace, the workaday normality of a busy city lying in the bright sunshine of a spring morning beneath the benevolent majesty of the Minster, itself lying behind the security of ancient fortified walls built against enemies of long, long ago . . .

'You, Timothy.'

The words seemed wrapped around by the moist redness of the lips. Casey, alias O'Phelan, smiled. 'Yes?'

'You have been listening to me?' The hint of steel: steel in the voice backed by steel in the shoulder-bag, where Casey knew she carried a gun. Casey smiled again. 'Sure I've been listening. Why would I not be?' He shifted in his seat, plumply, roundly: Casey was apple-cheeked and cheery looking, a comfortable man with a wife and family in a Dublin suburb: Timothy O'Phelan, however, was single—and single-minded for freedom, a fact that brought him strange bedfellows. Now he put on his Irish blandness, his native-expected blarney; his voice became soft, wheedling. 'Sure, I never would miss anything

6

you said, me darlin'—'

'Damn you, be serious!' The voice was a whip-lash. The girl leaned forward, her dark eyes alight with that strange brilliance. A hand tapped the table round which the five of them sat, like a committee, mundane in a mundane room. In the English city of York, it was incongruous that they should be discussing, mainly calmly and wholly objectively, the death of thousands and the paralysis of a capital. The girl continued, building up the picture, bringing the pieces, the last brush-strokes, together skilfully. Casey, closely attentive, knew one thing for sure: it was outlandish in its concept, in its aim, in its whole genesis—but it could work. The wonder in Casey's mind was that fanaticism hadn't got there months before, even years before when the various terrorist groups had started throwing their growing weight around the world.

★   ★   ★

The girl remained *in situ*, the four men left, but separately. Casey was the first to exit. He walked along the street of small terraced houses towards the main road out of York, the A59 to Green Hammerton and Harrogate. At the corner he turned right, heading for York's centre, past the shunting trains in the yard, over the railway bridge, whistling to himself. It was a long walk. Just short of Micklegate he turned left for the station. On the grassy slopes by the old city wall to his right, daffodils in profusion danced in the wind, turning their faces to the sun. *Daffodown-dilly, down the underground ... daffodown the steps to dillydeath*... Casey gave a cold grin and shook himself free of daft thoughts. Overhead light puffy clouds blew, scudding away to shadow the grandeur of the Dales in the north–west. Casey turned into the railway station, retrieved O'Phelan's hand-case from the Left Luggage, and bought a one-way second class ticket for King's Cross. Then he bought a paperback from the bookstall and went through the barrier for the London train. Idly he watched groups of train-spotting youngsters clustering at the ends of the long platforms that stretched away beyond the graceful curve of the glass-paned canopy. Casey was thinking of the olive-skinned girl: she was a good-looker all right, and bad for his immortal soul. He felt sorry for her, a sorrow that loomed large. She was not basically criminal, though her projected crime was of itself bigger by far than all the crimes committed by hardened criminals in the ordinary sense ever since the Bow Street Runners. Like so many other people, like so many of his own people, she was following an ideal. Casey shook his head with an immensity of regret: she was too vital, too full of sheer magnetism, too bloody attractive, to end up as dead meat at the busy end of a copper's gun or—worse perhaps—inside Holloway for upwards of thirty years. Casey gave a heavy sigh and watched the London-bound train slide in from Newcastle, chased by a rush of small boys. Climbing aboard, he found a corner seat, shoved his hand-case on the rack, and settled down to read. He read all the way to King's Cross, whence he took a tube, with more than usual interest and concern, to Piccadilly Circus. In the Regent Palace Hotel he checked into a room already booked in the name of Mr O'Phelan. In his room he opened the hand-case and unpacked the few contents. At six o'clock he went down to the hotel's Stetson Bar and bought himself a large Scotch. While he drank, he watched without appearing to do so: no familiar faces. At six fifteen he had an early snack meal: and at six forty he left the hotel by the door opening from the Stetson Bar. He went back to the Piccadilly underground—the bloody thing, he thought irritably, held some sort of fascination now—and took a train to Holborn, in the tail end of the rush hour. At Holborn he ascended the elevator humming the Londonderry Air to himself, quietly, full of thoughts of death. He walked to a line of telephone kiosks, found them all full of dolly-birds making dates, and decided it was better not to hang around. Emerging into

Kingsway, he turned south and walked down towards the Aldwych, stopping now and then to gaze in a shop window and carry out a careful rearward reconnaissance. Nothing alarming— again, no familiar faces. But the only telephone kiosks free had been, not unexpectedly, vandalised. He cursed under his breath, walked on, and eventually found his goal, free and in working order, a minor miracle on the Embankment. From memory well implanted he called a number that was not in the telephone directory and contacted Detective Chief Superintendent Simon Shard.

*   *   *

The Berserk Strip Club, behind its many barriers crossable only by continual pound-note proffering, was well enough named. Despite new laws, despite prosecutions and general police vigilance, the girls, as nude as ever, contorted and gyrated with abandon. Simon Shard, sunk in semi-darkness and anonymity, watched with the sardonic interest of a man whose own sex life was perfectly satisfactory: and watched with half an eye only, the other one and a half being on the entry through which he expected Detective Sergeant Casey of the Garda to appear. And his mind was running on much deeper lines than strip, lines deep down beneath London all mixed up with sewers and gas pipes and electricity cables and what-have-you: the mind boggled rather sharply at the havoc that any explosion deep below London would be sure to cause—and that, quite apart from the human element. Casey had said, this was to be big. *The biggest yet, four men to carry the explosives*. And where? How many miles of track did London's underground system nourish? Shard, off-hand, didn't know, but made a guess around three hundred miles. In the clammy atmosphere of eroticism and panting breath, Shard sweated and thought with great sincerity: thank God for Detective Sergeant Casey! With luck, his information should lead authority to a killing in plenty of time.

He looked at his watch: eight thirty-five. He wanted to be away home, found himself growing restless at eight forty. Even after Casey showed, he would have to contain his impatience a while longer: Casey couldn't leave straight away. He could and would grow bored after fifteen minutes or so—he knew the ropes—and then he would up and go, and half a minute later so would Shard. Simple ... but Beth called. Sometimes Shard thought of himself as a bum copper: too many wife-thoughts. The best coppers had harder shells.

At nine o'clock Casey had still not showed. Shard grew alarmed, but held his hand. Casey

11

could have slipped on a banana skin, Casey could have got himself lost in darkest London. But at nine forty-five Shard got up and left, looked out for Detective Sergeant Casey all the way down the alley outside, and knew he couldn't go home yet. He went back to his office in Seddon's Way and rang the Yard, which was a place where his word was still listened to with attention. He told the Yard just enough, and asked for a check. Then, this time personally, he called Beth and said he was desperately sorry. After that, the long wait and the nail-biting and the total inability to fill in the time by doing any routine paper-work. It was dawn by the time the Yard called him back and he almost knocked the telephone off his desk in his hurry to grab it.

'Shard . . .'

'Anstey, sir.'

'Well?'

'Bad news, sir. A body answering the description has turned up in the Thames off Wapping. Medical evidence suggests death occurred at about nine o'clock last night—'

'Drowning?'

'Not drowning, sir. Bleeding from wounds received. The private parts, sir. They've been excised, cut right off.' There was a pause, a cough. 'It's a habit of the Arabs, sir, I believe.'

Shard pulled himself together, tried not to see images of Casey, Casey who had really had no need to get himself involved initially, Casey of the Dublin Garda ... he said, 'Thank you, Anstey, I'll be in touch,' and then he rang off and sat staring at the wall ahead of his desk.

CHAPTER TWO

Old edifices seemed to age in crusted dignity, present-day buildings merely to become dirty and tawdry: the Foreign Office—that place of dignity in so much more positive a sense than new New Scotland Yard could ever be—had tended, ever since the first day of his appointment, both to impress and depress Simon Shard whenever he was called there from the anonymity of his crummy little office among the prostitutes of Seddon's Way. His boss, who was not and never had been a policeman, had a precisely similar effect: the Winchester and New College background, grouted in by the training of diplomacy, was bound to impress with its product, but Shard was saddened by other aspects of the man known as Hedge. Hedge was not his name, but was descriptive enough of his function, standing as he did between the sheltered VIP who was the actual Head of Security and the common herd beyond the pale. Hedge was a man of infinite capacity for self-preservation, as well able to adapt to the shears as any other hedge and to grow again thicker than before. Hedge could be relied upon to twist and turn in any corner and to contrive his way out; and was ever on his guard to spot any such Hedge-trapping corners before they fully materialised, just in case.

As this morning.

Hedge, pink and puffy, waved a nicely manicured hand at Shard. 'I don't understand. Just don't understand.'

'I'm trying to explain, Hedge.' Shard's tone was patience itself, though he wanted badly to take pink plumpness by its fleshy ruff, and shake. 'Detective Sergeant Casey—'

'Should never have been here in the first place—'

'But—'

'Or anyway—not within *our* ambit, Shard.' The waving intensified. 'Interpol—Scotland Yard—Special Branch—anyone you care to name. *Not us!* We are never seen to be involved—can't you take that in? What the devil am I to say to the Head of Department—have you thought of that, Shard?'

'How about the truth, Hedge?'

Round eyes opened wide. 'The truth?'

'It's the opposite of a lie.'

Hedge snapped, 'Don't be impertinent.'

'I apologise.'

'You're still too much the policeman, Shard. Too much ... beat and bobby—that's it—beat

14

and bobby!' Hedge looked almost coy, proudly diffident originator of the telling phrase. 'You must remember this is the Foreign Office, in a sense it's—'

'Unaccustomed to the truth, Hedge? No, just listen to me.' Shard leaned forward in his chair, staring Hedge into silence. Across Parliament Square, Big Ben struck the hour: ten o'clock. Casey had been dead thirteen hours, give or take a little: Shard had seen the body, a horrible sight, even the face mutilated so that recognition had been almost impossible. Even now, Shard felt sick ... a few seconds late on Big Ben, the rather pansy looking French clock on Hedge's mantelpiece also began its strike, beating softly out over well-polished mahogany and comfortably worn leather. Shard's voice rose above the combination of bells. 'Hedge, this is too big for brushing under any carpets. I reported to you ... oh, more than a couple of weeks back, that I was on to this. Casey was an old friend, I'd worked with him in my Yard days on jobs that involved London and the Republic. I—'

'When you reported, you never once spoke of Casey, Shard.'

'No. I admit that—and the reason was, at that time I didn't know Casey had come in on it. Once I did know, well, there seemed no reason for a special mention to you, Hedge. I'm entitled to run the show my way, the details are

15

up to me. Casey had come in virtually by mistake—he was investigating an IRA job, and he picked up something else. He—'

'Is the IRA involved?'

'Not in this, no. Casey told me that positively when he first got in touch. The IRA's in the clear, and I suspect the involvement of Middle Eastern terrorists—'

'*Why* do you suspect them?'

Shard lifted his shoulders. 'I suppose simply because they're the only other logical side of the terrorist coin. Also, of course, the way Casey died.'

Hedge nodded, said distastefully, 'The private parts, yes. Terrible! What a world we live in, to be sure. I believe they've even reinstated the old Islamic law—burial to the neck and stoning of adulterers, then the ploughing off of the head with a harrow.' Hedge shuddered, as though in danger himself, then came back to Whitehall. 'What do we tell Dublin, Shard?'

'Officially—I expect you're going to say—nothing. Aren't you?'

Hedge studied his fingernails. 'Well...'

'Unofficially,' Shard said, coming to his rescue, 'I'll go over and see Mr McCrory.'

'The Garda chief himself?' Hedge looked up, staring.

'Why not, Hedge? Or do *you* want to go?'

'Oh, no, no.' Hedge waved his arms again,

almost frantically dismissing the suggestion. 'It seems a good idea, I suppose, for you to go, but be careful what you say.'

'I'll do that,' Shard promised, 'but I'll also ask some questions, see if I pick up some leads—'

'Be careful in that direction too.'

'Of course. But from now on, Hedge, speed's got to be the keynote. We have ten days—nine, now. I suppose you do realise that.'

'Yes.' The pink man brought out a white linen handkerchief and dabbed beads of sweat from his forehead. 'But surely the situation's changed now?'

'Casey?'

'Yes. He was killed for a purpose, someone knew he'd talked. That being so—'

'They'll reshape the plan? Well, could be, of course. We can't rely on that, though, Hedge, can we? The counter-planning is bound to postulate the only known date ... but of course we must also assume it may now come *earlier*. We'll have to be ready as of now.'

Hedge blew out his cheeks. 'And are we?'

'Of course not.'

'Then—'

'Everything that has to be done, will be done, and as fast as I know how.'

Hedge nodded, sighed, looked at his French clock. 'I shall be seeing the Head of Department shortly. He'll need to be briefed

17

for his report to the Minister—and the Cabinet, I dare say. You may be wanted yourself—in person.' He looked fixedly at Shard. 'Tell me: do you believe this thing is *really* on?'

Shard said, 'I've no doubts at all—none. Casey was positive.'

Hedge groaned, shook his head. 'We must absolutely ensure it doesn't get out, Shard. The Press, you know!' Hedge, speaking of his number one enemy with bated breath, drummed plump fingers on the opulent leather top of his desk. 'We can't risk that—you can imagine the panic—London would come to a dead stop—'

Shard interrupted with a harsh laugh. 'Dead's the word, Hedge! A sizable explosion in the underground network, in a confined space … it wouldn't be pretty—'

'And just the thought of it, about to happen they don't know when—you've said it might be earlier … no, they'd all keep out of the tubes and off the streets even—' Hedge broke off. 'A thought, Shard: what's the given date again?'

'May the fourth.'

'I suppose we could close the underground that day, a last-minute thing?'

Shard lifted his hands in the air. 'We may have to, if it hasn't happened earlier, but it would be fairly pointless. We'd have to shut down the system permanently, wouldn't we, once we started? Unless we put the stopper on at once, they'll live to blow another day.'

'Yes . . . well, what are your proposals for the work-out, Shard?'

'I'll go to Dublin, then to York. I'll talk to London Transport—'

'Carefully, please. With circumspection. I do not, repeat not, wish anything to get about at this stage.'

'I take your point, but they can't be left out, as well you know—'

'But at this stage—'

'Even at this stage, Hedge. Oh, I'll be careful, don't worry! I'll feed them some line or other that'll give me maps and a full run-down on the organisation, the operating procedures and security arrangements. In the meantime, I'll need Yard and Special Branch co-operation in a search nationwide. I'll co-ordinate the toothcomb.' Shard paused, eyeing Hedge speculatively. 'Anything else on your mind?'

Hedge looked down at his desk. 'Casey.'

'And again the Press?'

'Exactly. There are to be no releases in regard to Casey. In the first instance, the Yard reacted splendidly. It's to stay that way. Get the body to Dublin, Shard, as secretly as you know how.' The eyes flickered. 'I'm sure you'll agree, that's only wise?' He looked up at Shard hopefully, chin dragging his mouth down: he looked like a sad salmon.

'As you say, Hedge—only wise.'

Shard got to his feet and left Hedge flicking a switch in his intercom and looking white around the gills as he negotiated an interview with the next God up the hierarchy. Only wise? Shard grinned without humour, a hard and savage grin towards Hedge's private fears. Wise it might be in one respect, since the Press, if they got hold of it, would trumpet loudly about any involvement of an Irish copper on British soil and under the aegis of the British Foreign Office; and all security *vis-à-vis* the terrorists would vanish in a puff of smoke. On the other hand, the terrorists themselves would know well enough whom they had killed . . . while, on yet another hand, they might not know how much Casey had said before he died. Shard, moving along the quiet dignity of the Foreign Office corridors for the ground floor exit, pondered: maybe a clampdown on Casey had its points, could help to keep the other side guessing. The body could be reported as found but unidentified, which should keep Hedge happy. Reaching his office, Shard called the FO switchboard, asking them to get first the Yard and then Dublin on the security line.

★   ★   ★

Hesseltine, Assistant Commissioner Crime, was an old Yard colleague. 'On your word, Simon, I'll do it,' he said.

'Thank you, sir. I'd say, let the Press have the details of—how it was done, where the body was found, and nothing else at all. Just nothing.'

'A police spokesman said, enquiries were being made. That do?'

'Admirably, sir.'

'How about transport to Dublin?'

Shard said, 'I'll fix, don't worry. The only other thing I'm asking is that you hold off the Press for at least nine days as of now.'

'Right! You're putting me in a spot over the inquest, though, Simon.'

Shard grinned into the mouthpiece. 'Sorry about that, but I'm sure you'll find a way out. I'd like to emphasise—and don't tell me I'm beginning to sound like Hedge—that the national consideration now overrides all else. The coroner will have to lump it.'

'All right, all right. By the way, how's Hedge taking it?'

'Fearfully, as usual.'

From the other end of the line a chuckle sounded. Hesseltine loathed Hedge's guts. Shard cut the call and waited for Dublin to come on. When it did so, he informed McCrory personally that he was coming over on a private flight and would appreciate an interview as soon as possible after his arrival, which would be after dark—at ten o'clock approximately. He added, sounding casual, that he would be grateful if a closed van with a plain clothes escort could meet his plane at Dublin airport. This fixed, Shard took himself to St James's Park station and had a long session with a top man from London Transport's security section. His approach was cautious, turning the points of the security officer's probes.

'It's a general check,' he said smoothly.

'Nothing more specific, Chief Superintendent?'

'Not so far as I can say. Your tracks, your stations—they're vulnerable. Always have been ... no harm in having a preliminary survey, you know. We aim to prevent trouble before it comes, and to do that we need to be genned up well in advance.'

'Yes, quite.' Partington, the security man, gnawed at his bottom lip. 'If there was any direct threat that you knew of ... you'd give us the word?'

Shard nodded. 'Yes, we would.'

'In good time?'

Shard thought of those nine days and met Partington's eye. 'We would give you,' he said, 'all the warning we could and that's a promise. But even we can be caught with our pants round our ankles.' He paused, then asked reflectively, 'Suppose there was some positive knowledge of a threat ... say a bomb, its whereabouts not known. What would you do about it?'

'Well, in the first place, we'd obviously liaise with your people, wouldn't we?'

'Yes. But what would your advice be—knowing your system as you do?'

Partington drew in a long breath, sent it whistling out again. 'Our advice ... taking it that you would have no idea of any region, however broad, where this hypothetical bomb might be?'

'Right.'

Partington said, 'A shutdown. A complete shutdown.'

'And then a full search by police and army explosives experts, which could take a hell of a long time—but I've no doubt it would be the only way,' Shard said briskly. 'And now, if I could take a look at your network maps, and then go into the security arrangements...'

★   ★   ★

Shard's flight was to be from Shoreham airport in Sussex; he left the Foreign Office in a government car with driver, after a quick visit home to tell Beth he would be back in the morning. Just beyond Lambeth Town Hall, on the A23 Brighton road, Shard's car picked up the plain van that was carrying the body of Detective Sergeant Casey. They overtook, but kept it in sight in the rear-view mirror as best they could. Turning onto the A24 and making

23

for the Leatherhead by-pass, Shard's driver slowed to allow the makeshift hearse to catch up. They drove into Shoreham airport at eight thirty, the van going straight into a hangar, where Shard's plane was waiting. Under cover of the hangar, Casey's body was transferred aboard and the van drove off, Shard's car following it fifteen minutes later, by which time Shard was airborne and heading out west and a little north for Dublin. Enfolded by the engine's roar, alone with the silent body, Shard sat thinking, thinking largely of Detective Sergeant Casey, an Irishman and a Republican who had, in essence, died for England; or anyway, for more Londoners than Shard wanted to visualise. Casey had left a wife and two children—Shard had met them. Casey had been a cheerful man and carefree, happily married, and now there was to be no happiness in the Casey home. Shard knew it was up to him to visit—to visit and if possible comfort, and at the same time to talk of silence. Before leaving London, he had seen the evening papers. Such was the day and age that the finding of the mutilated body had made no headlines—Hedge would be glad about that at all events—and not a lot of mention: some man unknown had met his end in a particularly brutal fashion and the body had been thrown into the Thames. That was that, and no more need be heard—except that some of the

24

Sundays would titillate their readers with the sexual details—until after the whole thing had been bowled out and cleared up.

CHAPTER THREE

McCrory was, in comparison with Casey, the other type of Irishman: tall and dark, with plenty of five o'clock shadow and a long upper lip, cadaverous where Casey had been round and lively, and introvert where Casey had been extrovert. McCrory gloomed at Shard.

'It's my responsibility so far as this end is concerned, Mr Shard. I gave permission—to my regret now. It's a nasty business.'

'Very nasty.' Shard coughed: time was too short, or could be, for general comment on beastliness. 'The widow, Mr McCrory. What do we tell her?'

'The truth is no bad thing.'

Shard, having said something similar himself back in London, thought of Hedge. 'We don't want a common London–Dublin involvement reported in the papers, sir, taking into account the nature of my job. I'm sure a way can be found. My chief would appreciate that, I know.'

McCrory's gloom seemed to deepen. 'Hedge, Mr Shard?'

'Yes.'

'I know Hedge. I'm not unsympathetic. I'm not unsympathetic towards England either, as you know. I don't want to see harm come to London. But Casey was one of my officers, and now he's left three people in my care, Mr Shard. I have a regard for the truth.'

'So have I, but . . .'

'But what?'

Shard met the Garda chief's eye squarely. 'On the flight in, sir, it came to me that Casey would—keep. On ice, I mean.'

There was a silence, then McCrory said, 'I think you're a hard man, Mr Shard—oh, I know we all have to be that at times and it's London and not Dublin that's threatened by these terrorists.' He paused. 'What do they want, do you suppose?'

Shard shrugged. 'Apparently nothing. There haven't been any demands so far—they could come, of course, but I've an idea they won't. We haven't any of their own people in custody, nor anyone else I can think of that they might have an interest in. It's just going to happen regardless.'

'So it's just a kind of large-scale vandalism?'

'Yes, in a sense, I think it is. Politically linked in the broad aspect, of course. They want to keep the Western nations living in fear, wondering what's going to happen next, until all their own national problems are sorted out.'

McCrory gave a tight smile. 'You English took on too much, years ago. Now you're suffering for it from many directions. This time you seem to be saying you don't suspect the IRA, either the Provos or—'

'That's right.'

McCrory nodded, seeming satisfied, but asked, 'Just on account of the private parts, Mr Shard, is this?'

'Not that alone. Casey had been in touch before. He didn't know much then, but he did positively confirm a Middle Eastern basis—'

'But they were glad enough of his help, as a supposed Provo?'

'Yes. He met open arms and I gather not a lot of checking. These people are rather naïve, you know, Mr McCrory. They think in absolute terms—guns and bombs and the universal brotherhood of terrorism.'

'Even so, something went wrong for Casey. And now you're asking me to keep him on ice, by which I take it you're asking me to keep the news of his death on ice too—and not even to tell the wife. Why, Mr Shard?'

'Because a sorrowing wife and children will not easily be kept out of the way of the Press, sir.'

'That could be arranged.'

'With respect, sir, no arrangement could be 100 percent reliable. And so far as possible we don't want the villains to be absolutely certain

27

we've identified Casey. We—'

'Can you hold back on that?'

'We shall try. There were facial mutilations as well as the others . . . and of course he carried nothing to identify him for what he was—'

'Quite, yes.'

'We don't want to react, because we—or at any rate *I*—have just a notion that our terrorists may not know Casey talked.'

'But I understood you to say—'

'I know what I said, sir, but I know something else as well: I knew Tom Casey. Do you follow what I'm trying to say?'

McCrory's brows had gone up, arching over the long, dark face. He asked in a controlled voice, 'Are we back to the private parts again, Mr Shard?'

Shard nodded. 'Right. I say again, I knew Tom Casey.'

'He was a good Catholic, Mr Shard.'

'Agreed. Many good Catholics are also full-blooded men, and some good Catholics are better than others at containment. Tom Casey always had an eye for a dolly bird and it does no good to disguise the fact—nor should we forget that so many Middle Eastern girls are very attractive, physically, to us Westerners. There's something else we shouldn't forget—'

'The private parts?'

Again Shard nodded. 'Exactly. That strikes me as being more personal than in the line of duty. I'd like to find out more about it if I can.'

'And can you?'

'I think so. But not from the wife, fairly obviously. And I repeat, I don't want it known, if it's not known already, that Casey talked. There's one person I would expect to be able to trust implicitly.'

'And he is?'

Shard paused, taking a deep breath and holding the Garda chief's eyes in his own gaze. Then he said, 'Mr McCrory, I'm going to ask you to give me the name of Tom Casey's parish priest.'

★   ★   ★

It was a battle, hard fought and argued. The priest, McCrory avowed, would not and could not break the confessional. Pacifically Shard agreed but said it was worth a try even so: the priest could always say no, it would be entirely up to him and no pressure would be applied. McCrory's views would be passed on faithfully. McCrory said the confessional was customarily anonymous. Again Shard agreed, knowing that this was not invariably so and feeling that a policeman, if confessing about something that impinged on a duty assignment of the nature of this one, would make his confession in the privacy of the presbytery, for even churches could hold hidden ears. In the end Shard won.

29

McCrory even lent him a plain car and a plain-clothes Garda driver to speed him through the Dublin streets to the suburb where Casey had lived. Old Dublin, the spacious city that had once known the rule of the Lord Lieutenancy, the Union Flag flying over its government buildings until the final culmination in 1922 of the long fighting that had changed the face of Ireland, faded into modern bungalow town, incongruous, in daylight at all events, under the distant backdrop of the Wicklow Mountains. The church was as new as the bungalows, built of brick with a conical bell-tower and the presbytery adjoining snugly.

Shard told his driver to wait, and walked up a gravel path to a small porch, where he rang a bell. An old woman, bent and wrinkled, came after some delay: a crone from the west of Ireland, Shard fancied, who not so long ago would have worn the shawl and was even now dressed entirely in black: one of the faithful, maybe, who had accompanied the Father from some earlier cure of souls?

'Yes?' she asked in a creaking, ancient voice. 'Who is it, then?'

'Is Father Donnellan in?'

'He is. Who are you?'

Shard said, 'Someone in need of help. Does the Father need to know more than that?'

The old woman sniffed. 'I dare say not,

though if it was me, sure I'd send the half of yer packin'. Tis confessions and advice, confessions and advice mornin', noon and night till the poor man never has time for a meal let alone get to his bed.' She opened the door wider. 'Come in with yer then, tis a cold night for the time of the year. Wait in the hall till I tell the Father.'

Beady black eyes, brilliant in the hall light, stared at him. The old woman banged the door shut and went off muttering under her breath, her black-stockinged legs twinkling along with astonishing agility. She knocked on a door, spoke, turned and beckoned to Shard, who felt as guilty as any sinner. 'Come along then,' she called shrilly, 'and don't keep the Father away too long from his sleep.'

Shard approached the open door of a study, furnished contemporarily but comfortably. To his surprise, the priest was not old as he had somehow expected: he was a youngish man, no more than in his late twenties, with a friendly smile and fashionably long fair hair that fell to the clerical black of his coat collar. Shard smiled. 'Father Donnellan?'

'That's right. How can I help you?'

'That may take some time to explain. First, you'll want to know who I am—'

'Not if you don't want to tell me.'

'Oh?' Shard felt a small shock of surprise, but went on, 'No, I shall tell you, though I'll ask you to keep this visit to yourself, Father

Donnellan.' He explained his status, making a reference to the Garda chief. The priest raised his eyebrows, but didn't comment. Shard said, 'You'll understand that my edict doesn't run in this country but—'

'You're off your patch, Chief Superintendent?'

'Er—yes, you might say so, indeed!'

'And you've not come to me to confess?' the priest asked, smiling.

'No, I—'

'In that case,' Father Donnellan said cheerfully, 'sit down and join me in a nightcap. Whisky?'

'Thank you, yes.'

'It's Scotch, I'm afraid, not Irish. It's unpatriotic of me, but I got the taste when I was in London.'

'You've been in London, then?'

The priest nodded, and moved across to the cupboard. 'I was one of the many clergy at Westminster Cathedral. So I know your manor fairly well, Mr Shard.' He came back with a decanter, a soda syphon and two crystal tumblers. When he had poured two stiff glasses, he cocked an eye at Shard. 'Well? What do you want of me, Mr Shard?'

Shard came direct to the point. 'I'm seeking vital information, and I mean vital. A lot of lives may be at stake. I'm going to ask you, Father, to break the vows of the confessional.'

32

The priest smiled. 'In that case, Mr Shard, I'm afraid you've had a long journey for absolutely nothing. I take it, of course, you're not a Catholic. But I'd have thought you'd have known all the same.'

'Yes, I do know. I'm very sorry to have to ask you this, believe me. Mr McCrory doesn't approve and was certain you would not help. He could be right, and I have no means, even if I wished to use them, of making you do what you don't want to do. That's understood.'

Donnellan nodded, frowning. 'Why not sit down?' he said.

'Thank you.' Shard sat in a curious-looking whitewood chair with a small table by its side. He placed the whisky tumbler on this table: the priest sat opposite him and said, 'You don't look to me an irreligious man. A priest can tell, you know. Many policemen do have that look, the stupid, bullying look, but not you. That may not be a compliment to a policeman, but it's meant as such.'

Shard smiled. 'Thank you!'

'You spoke of something being vital, and of—I think—lives at risk. Have you come on a junkie hunt?'

'No, not that at all. This is—something very much more immediate that may involve the deaths of very many people within the next few days. Time's that short! We would very much appreciate any help you can give us, Father.'

'Can you be more precise?' The priest paused. 'No?'

'I'm afraid not.'

'I see. But, you know, you haven't framed a question yet! Don't let the cloth put you off, nor even the confessional. We men of God, Mr Shard, are worldly enough beneath the dog-collar—and we do hear things that aren't covered by any vows.'

Shard inclined his head gratefully. 'Thank you again, Father. My first question is this: do you have in your parish a Garda officer named Casey?'

'I think you know I have, or you wouldn't have come.'

'Right! I do know. Can you tell me, is he in the habit of confessing to you, Father Donnellan?'

'He's a good Catholic. You may infer from that ... what you wish.'

'Very well,' Shard said, smiling, 'I have inferred! Now, here's the hard part, or anyway the start of it. What I say must not be repeated, please.' He occupied himself with his whisky tumbler but, under cover of this, watched the face of the priest with immense care and concentration. 'Tom Casey was a good friend of mine and Tom Casey's dead. Murdered very horribly.'

The priest's head jerked up, the eyes widening: Shard was convinced the reaction was natural, that the news had shocked. 'No!'

'I'm afraid, yes. Currently, we don't know who did it. We have no leads, none at all. He was working on something he didn't need to work on but wanted to, because he wanted to save lives. Now, only you can do that—or may be able to. Not being a Catholic, I don't know if the confessional holds its sanctity after death—'

'Then let me assure you, it does.'

'I see,' Shard said in a flat tone. 'In that case, you'll not be able to tell me if a woman had come into Tom Casey's life. A woman that he may have told you about ... a woman that he would not wish his wife to hear of.'

'A woman?' The priest's eyes had narrowed, and he was looking more than ever troubled: Shard felt he had scored a point. He got to his feet, his face hard now.

He said, 'Yes, a woman. The way Tom died...' In a few words, he described the injuries as reported by the Yard. 'Father, you must be aware of Arab customs. They aren't pretty! This speaks to me of the involvement of a woman, an Arab woman, and if we knew who she was, then we would have a good lead. Father, Tom Casey's dead.' Shard was sweating now, his voice urgent. 'Do you really think it will offend your God and mine if you help to find his killers—if by so doing you save so many more innocent lives, the lives of men, women and children, many of whom will be Catholics

35

like yourself, even perhaps former colleagues—if that's the word—at Westminster Cathedral? *Do you?*'

He mopped at his face, was surprised, when he looked again, to find Father Donnellan smiling. The priest said, 'Oh, there's no vow involved. Tom Casey was a realist, you know, and honest with it. Not for him the sinning, and then the confession, and then the sinning again! When he came to me, he came as a friend in search of advice and comfort, not as a priest. His confessions were genuine ones, when he made them, and those sins were not repeated after forgiveness. He talked to me about his special weakness *outside* the confessional.'

'So there was a woman?'

'There were several women—I say this in confidence, of course, and never mind the non-confessional nature—'

'Yes—'

'His wife must never know. I trust you with the information, which broadly perhaps you knew already—'

'Yes, I did. The name of the most recent woman, Father?'

'A striking one. Tom said she was a striking woman too! The name—Nadia Nazarrazeen.'

Shard blew out a releasing breath. 'For that I thank you, Father Donnellan! Did Tom ever say anything else—about his work perhaps, anything that—'

'Would lead you to Miss Nazarrazeen? No, he didn't. I don't think you'd have expected him to. I've no idea how or where or why they met—' Very suddenly, the priest broke off. In the silence that followed his upraised hand, Shard heard a sound, a small one, from the hall outside: like a faint cry, quickly stifled. Before Shard could move to stop him, Father Donnellan had run across to the door and jerked it open. What followed was like some sort of sleight-of-hand: now you saw him, now you didn't. There was the shattering roar of a gun, three times rapidly repeated, a belch of acrid-smelling gunsmoke. Behind the door, the priest fell, reeling, clutching at his throat, breath rasping. As the body fell out of sight behind the door, Shard, his own revolver in his hand now, slid towards the jamb and looked through: a hooded man stood there, a big man with brilliant eyes visible behind slits in the canvas hood, a man engaged in kicking death out of his way into the study.

CHAPTER FOUR

Shard was lucky in one way, unlucky in another: his reaction was fast, almost too fast. He fired blindly through the panel of the study door, and the heavy bullet of the Smith and

37

Wesson Chief's Special hit flesh. There was a kind of gargling cry and something thumped back against the door, smashing it against Shard. Shard came out from cover and saw the man on the floor, lying half across the body of the parish priest; and saw the widening stain, the thick ooze of blood welling up and out from around the waistband of check-patterned bell-bottoms.

He bent and felt for the beat of hearts: Father Donnellan was stone cold dead, the hooded man lived still but wasn't going to last long. In the meantime he was in no condition to talk: the mouth hung slack when Shard dragged off the hood, the eyes seemed already glazing. Breathing was heavy, stertorous. And the skin was brown, the features Arabic, classic Arabic of hooked nose, black eyes, thick brows, black moustache and beard. Maybe things were starting to jell, but the flavour hadn't yet become apparent; and it was a thousand pities the man with the hood was going to die before he could talk.

Shard picked up the murder weapon from where it had fallen: oddly, it was a Uzi—a sub-machine-gun of Israeli make. Uzis were good: compact too—9mm, 25-round magazine, detachable, with a sliding metal stock, 25 inches extended, 9lbs loaded weight. The magazine was in the right-hand grip and a grip-safe stopped it blasting off if dropped. Shard wondered about the Uzi: a trophy from one of the nine-day-wonder Israeli–Arab wars, or simple thieving? Whatever the origin, that Uzi could talk after the death of its owner, but what it had to say would depend upon whether or not the fingerprint sections at the Foreign Office, Special Branch or the Yard's CRO had the filed wherewithal to interpret. Laying down the gun Shard went across for Father Donnellan's telephone: not unexpectedly, the line was dead. Moving back fast for the door, Shard stepped over the bodies and went out into the hall. Here it was quiet, but a door stood open at the back end. Gun in hand, Shard advanced. He kicked back the door savagely and it rebounded in his face, bouncing off more death: a hummock of faded black—the old woman, garrotted, with a bootlace tight-knotted around the flabby, wrinkled neck. As he bent to the body the front door opened behind him and he came upright, gun ready: but it was the driver of the police car, looking dead scared.

'Are you all right, sir?'

'I'm all right.' Shard gestured down at the bodies. 'Get a plain van, no fuss.'

The driver turned away; Shard stopped him. 'Didn't you see anyone approaching the presbytery?'

'I did not, sir. Not a thing.'

'No cars parked after we did?'

'No, sir.'

'All right, off you go. I'll wait. Fast as you can.' The policeman went out and Shard followed. He looked around: as the man had said, no cars. The gunman could have parked anywhere in bungalow-ville and then walked.

★   ★   ★

'It's being taken *very* seriously,' Hedge said at four o'clock next afternoon on the security line to Seddon's Way. 'The Cabinet's meeting in half an hour and you'll be required to attend with me. Is—'

'Use your influence, Hedge. Prevent a hoo-ha.'

'Hoo-ha?'

'You know what I mean: we do not, repeat not, want a full-scale operation yet. I want to lull them—they still may not know Casey was in contact—'

'No? Then how d'you explain a tail being put on you?'

Shard whistled through his teeth. 'We don't know it was a tail. Personally I don't believe it was. If we assume it was, then we must assume Casey actually talked—under some nasty pressure. I don't believe Casey would do that. On the other hand, Casey used to grow maudlin when he'd had a drink. Maudlin in a *religious* sense, Hedge. Are you with me?'

Hedge snapped, 'No, I'm not!'

40

'The priest, Hedge, Casey's priest. They'd have known he was a Catholic for a start. They could have had just the same idea as me. Now d'you get it?'

'So they silenced the priest?'

'Exactly. Just in case. Not knowing I'd got there first.'

There was a grunt along the wire. Hedge asked, 'Anything fresh on the hooded man?'

'Nothing. I was about to ring you ... all fingerprint sections report a blank, and as you know already, that includes Dublin and Belfast—'

'The body—the man himself—'

'No identification.'

'He's absolutely not known in Ireland?'

'I told you. No Garda or RUC knowledge at all, not that I expected it.'

'So we're no further ahead?'

'Except for Nadia Nazarrazeen. That's important—'

'Yes, yes.' Hedge sounded stiff, as though he would have liked to reprimand Tom Casey: one day, Shard thought, the man would grow up. Even policemen felt the pangs of sex, though Hedge's view appeared to be that they had no right to. 'Poor show—that. On Casey's part, I mean—'

'Never mind the sex lectures, Hedge. This meeting: I'll come as ordered—'

'Of course you will—'

41

'—but I don't want to hang about, Hedge, because I'm going north this evening.'

'York?'

'Yes.'

'This—er—*woman*, Nazarrasomething?'

'Zeen. Yes.'

Hedge said disparagingly, 'Shard, do be careful, won't you?'

Shard grinned into the mouthpiece, icily. 'Oh, I will, don't worry. If you're concerned about my private parts, don't be. I'll not be making contact at this stage—' He stopped, grinning still. Hedge had hung up on him, slam bang. Shard sat back for a moment, rocking back on his chair-legs, arms at full stretch against his desk. He marshalled his thoughts, preparing for a grill from the Cabinet brass. Casey, Dublin, Donnellan, Nazarrazeen, a hooded Arab thug, four men to carry the explosives, and a pretty clear mental image, plus maps and statistics, of London's underground system. What he knew was little enough: it shouldn't take long to put bare facts across to the Cabinet. Shard's thoughts moved homeward to Beth, facing another night alone, with him chasing Arab dolly birds, if she did but know, in York. He left Seddon's Way and drove to Number 10, where the Cabinet meeting was to be held.

★ ★ ★

The brass was in full muster plus: some of them were not in fact Cabinet ministers. The P.M. sat fatly soft at the highly polished table, surveying Home Secretary, Minister of Defence, Secretary of the Environment, Foreign Secretary, the ministers concerned with health and housing and local government and a lot more. Also present as well as Hedge was Assistant Commissioner Hesseltine with his chief, and the chairmen of London Transport and the GLC. Full as the muster was, Shard had a strong and depressing feeling that the threat was in fact being taken less than duly seriously. A tall, thin man with thick glasses and a face like a corpse, a man whom Shard failed to identify, talked *sotto voce* to his neighbour all through the preliminaries: Shard, longing to shake him by the scraggy neck, heard him say something about terrorists being too familiar a part of the scene to get one's knickers in a twist about: the neighbour guffawed his agreement and proceeded to fix a round of golf at Sunningdale for the next day. Shard thought helplessly and with grinding teeth about Detective Sergeant Casey and Father Donnellan and others ...

He heard his name spoken by the Prime Minister: he stood up, notes in hand.

'Your full report, please, Chief Super-intendent.'

43

Shard gave it, fully factual, unemotional, concise: the thin man continued talking waggishly, behind his hand, and Shard seethed inside. When he had finished there was a silence, this time total, until the Prime Minister said 'Thank you. Your opinion, Chief Superintendent?'

'As to the reality, sir?'

'Yes.'

'It's real, sir. They mean it.'

'And can do it?'

Shard said, 'It's not impossible, sir. Security's faced with many problems when handling millions of commuters. If these people are able to place their bombs ... well, I've referred to what appears to be a large amount of explosive. Any large explosion in a confined space has immense potential. I've no doubt London Transport will confirm the dangers, and the possibilities.'

The Prime Minister sought the view of London Transport. 'Sir John?'

Sir John Ainsworth, heavy built, pugnacious, removed his glasses and dangled them from his fingers. He said, 'I do confirm. Lives and property—very much at risk. Lives especially, and that's what we're most concerned with, of course—'

'But property?'

Ainsworth shrugged. 'London's London! The whole network is heavily built over, as we

44

all know. It depends, naturally, on the size of the explosion, but ... well, I'm no explosives expert, but I would suggest that the force of any explosion such as we're talking of, would tend to dissipate laterally along the tunnel, rather than upwards against the strength of iron and the sand and cement grouting, plus the weight of London clay. Line of least resistance, don't you know—though I'd not care to be too dogmatic about this. Foundations could be shaken, and then there's all the other networks—gas, electricity, telephones, water ...'

'Sewage ...'

'Yes, sewage.' The discussion became more general, but Ainsworth's views as to lines of least resistance and the lateral spread gained support: it was pointed out that arch construction such as tunnelling was immensely strong, virtually indestructible. Shard, listening to the views and arguments, heard sense and nonsense mixed. And something nagged, though he couldn't have put a name to it other than to say that there had been some extra quality in Tom Casey's voice when he had made that call to Seddon's Way, something that spoke rather eloquently about something special, something that Shard felt went beyond a big bang in a tunnel or a train in motion. And there was another angle: terrorists were incalculable, were men of strange minds; extremists so often

45

seemed able to bring off extremes, things impossible to the moderates and the law-abiding. Because they were so incalculably and unpredictably unorthodox, they were so much harder to combat. Men of government were seldom fitted to cope, their minds were too rigidly set on fixed courses, working along those lines of orthodoxy and the expected, the lines of men who themselves were accustomed to follow the rule book. Always the vagabond had the advantage . . .

Graciously permitted to leave before any hard decisions were taken, Shard got into his car and headed for the M1. Utterances lingered in his mind: the Prime Minister, in saying that in his view the time had not yet come to alarm the public and in accepting Shard's plea to avoid panic action, had referred to the fact that for some while past the security services had been prepared for operations by Middle Eastern terrorists in London; they hadn't let any grass grow. And had said something else: 'We shall cope. You're our co-ordinator, Mr Shard. Ask, and you shall receive! At this stage, we're content to leave it in your hands. We know you'll be doing your best.'

Shard, inching through London's traffic, felt a momentary coldness: he'd asked for it, it was what he wanted, but it left no room for error. On his further word would depend Prime Ministerial decision and action, and that word mustn't come even a second too late. He pondered on his quarry, Nadia Nazarrazeen: he had nothing on her but the statement of Father Donnellan, now dead. Checks had produced the blankest blank ever: Home Office Immigration had no knowledge, nor had the FO's Passport Section, nor had the Yard, nor—scraping the bottom of the barrel—had Customs. Nor, another barrel-bottom, had the Dublin Garda or the Royal Ulster Constabulary, who had been asked to check this along with the prints on the Uzi. Yet Shard felt, more by an instinct that had seldom let him down than by cool reason, that Nadia Nazarrazeen was the key; though at the same time he had to admit that she could be in a separate compartment of Tom Casey's life, the purely love compartment. This he didn't believe—again for no very clear reason. Such reason as he found lay along perhaps shaky lines: Nadia Nazarrazeen *sounded* like a terrorist and had indisputably produced death—indisputably in Shard's book, anyhow. And again: Tom Casey, whose duty it had been to convince and infiltrate, may have found that to act naturally was the best way in, and Tom Casey's natural way was to make love.

★   ★   ★

Shard, with half his mind still on the possibility of tails however remote, watched carefully on the motorway but found nothing to arouse any suspicions. He took it fast, disdaining the service areas except for a stop for petrol at the last oasis before the M18. No worries, all the way into York. Unhopefully he made contact with the police: they had already reported to London by telex, no knowledge of any Nadia Nazarrazeen. Nevertheless, the one available fact remained, rock-like: Tom Casey had struck gold here in York. That had been a pretty short while ago: even if they had shifted base in that short interval, the villains must have left traces.

'What do you propose, Mr Shard?' the officer in charge asked him.

'I'll circulate.'

'That'll take time, won't it?'

'It's still the best way in my book.'

'I'd have thought that to concentrate on London ... you know what I mean, a watch on the stations—'

Shard interrupted with a laugh. 'That'll be done too—for what it's worth. Remember there are 279 stations all told. How do you stop determined terrorists getting to the target? Think of London's rush hour, or any time of day come to that! You can't check everyone for arms and explosives, and gentlemen from the Middle East are no rare flowers.'

The Superintendent rubbed at his chin. 'They hold all the cards, right enough—'

'Most of them, anyway. Once I get to Nadia

Nazarrazeen, I'll have a few of them myself—and I have a need to be fast. I'm not familiar with your patch, Superintendent. Can you give me a man who is?'

'I can, Mr Shard, but you'll appreciate that the clients will also be familiar with *him*—'

'I know. I want his words of wisdom, not his physical presence. Someone, maybe one of your DCs, who's close to the ground and what crawls in it.'

'I'll see to that right away,' the Superintendent said, lifting an internal telephone. All arrangements made, Shard had an idea.

'I don't need my car for what I'm going to do in York. In a sense this is gilding the lily ... don't tell me! But just in case my registration's been noted outside the nick, it wouldn't be a bad thing if I were seen to go back to London, all empty-handed. You've probably got someone near enough my shape on a dark night!'

★   ★   ★

The York police gave fullest co-operation: Shard had a long and useful talk with a DC who could have fooled anybody he was a genuine layabout. His information was comprehensive and included the address of a cellar used as a dosshouse by dropouts: his practical help

49

included items from the CID ragbag after a close and critical survey of Shard's own potentialities for fooling the fraternity.

'*Not* a hippie, sir.'

'Too old?'

The DC grinned. 'Well, sir, there *are* hippie daddies—'

'Not *that* old,' Shard snapped.

'No, but you want to be a hundred percent.'

'I told you, did I not—I want to be someone who knew Detective Sergeant Casey. How about an ex-con ... become one of the travelling gentry, a tramp?'

'Yes, that'd fit, sir. Nicked in the Republic?'

'It'd have to be that.'

'Can you do an Irish accent?'

Shard shook his head. 'Not to convince. It won't be necessary. The British do go to darkest Ireland, you know! I could have been on the run, couldn't I?'

'I reckon you could, sir, yes.' The DC studied Shard through half-closed eyes. 'A mixture of gear in that case: anything you could have picked up, plus overall filth and a smell of meths. We'll louse you up a bit.'

'Thanks very much,' Shard said, sounding bitter. He underwent the lousing process and when geared up didn't recognise himself in the mirror. Even the stench was genuine: the garments had come from very real tramps and the meths was straight from the bottle. Meths, stale urine and dried sweat made a horrible combination and Shard, when forcibly and convincingly ejected from the nick an hour or two later, was aware that the police were glad to see him go. Half an hour after ejection, as he made his horrible way along the ancient streets of York towards Monk Bar, his car ostentatiously headed Londonwards along the A64.

★   ★   ★

Shard got utterly lost: York was not an easy city for the visitor. He shambled, spreading stench, off course, past Whip-ma-Whop-ma Gate, found himself in a big oblong of shops, a wide thoroughfare. A uniformed constable watched, distantly from a corner: Shard reduced the shamble, glad of distance to dissipate the meths-smell. Moving on, he found his guide-line in the massive rearing eminence of the Minster, and headed for it as straight as possible, worrying about time and deadlines and thinking of horror in London's underground. Soon he found himself coming right down upon the Minster, with a pedestrian crossing leading to steps up to a massive door. He fumbled across the road, tattered garments flapping out in a light wind, was woefully conscious of the stares of passers-by, though these assured him that he was sailing under convincing colours. Along Deangate, then confidently left for Monk Bar. Shard lurched, muttering to himself and belching—he had actually drunk some meths for good measure as to his breath—under the bar, along the narrow pavements below the old city walls. A wild and undignified leap saved his life from a stream of traffic just beyond the bar, where he crossed the main road from Thirsk on the fringe of the North Yorkshire moors. Grumbling and muttering, almost convincing himself by now, he tottered on unkempt legs down a street of old moth-eaten buildings, looking out for his goal. He identified it quickly enough: a tall house, all windows boarded, clearly unoccupied except by, as he knew, the unsavoury. In the pavement in front of this house, which had seen far better days, was a sagging wooden cover over what had been a coal chute, a cover held from below by battens. Following instructions given at the nick, Shard approached this wooden cover and brought his foot down on it, three times followed after a pause by two more bangs. Then he mounted three cracked stone steps and repeated his message with a fist on the door.

He waited.

From far off inside the building came the sound of footsteps, dragging and uncertain. A few moments later the door opened. At first Shard saw no one in the intense dark, then he made out a man, very tall, a man who started to cough as clean air struck him.

'Who is it?' the man asked between coughs.

'Let me in, brother, I can't walk another step.' Shard blew meths, hopefully, but knew the aroma must lose the battle against what was coming from the interior. He almost retched as the tall man drew him inside and shut the door. He stood there in pitch darkness, darkness so thick that it seemed to muffle thought itself. He felt the tall man take his arm and urge him forward. Moving dead slow, feeling well ahead with his feet and his free arm, Shard moved, assailed by the smell of defeated humanity, of men and maybe women who had hit bottom and hit it hard. As he went, Shard felt oppression grow, and with it doubt: this horrible house might well be an operating base for him, but in all conscience it might be little more: in any society, you tended to stratify and to remain in the strata you rose to or descended to by natural selection—or the strata you chose for yourself. Once identified with the occupants of this house, with the deadbeats and the bums and the alcoholics, you might find it hard to make the contacts you wanted. The people who had killed Tom Casey, whatever else they were, could not come into the deadbeat category. The wires could after all fail to cross in time—and time was short.

Shard moved on, feeling trapped. From

somewhere beneath his feet, a scream sounded suddenly—horrible, chilling, a maniac sound of hell-fire followed by a sobbing that rose and fell.

Beside him, the tall man, invisible but tangible, said nothing.

CHAPTER FIVE

He was bedded down on some sacks and newspapers, no questions asked. His neighbours on either side were close, and slept disturbingly and noisily, breathing through organ pipes, yattering from time to time, lashing out with legs and arms. The screaming and the sobbing continued intermittently. Shard felt sick from the smell, which was made up of very many elements, all of them human. Not till the light of morning, coming dimly through the cracks around the wooden cellar cover, outlined the room, did Shard actually see his companions. Hair, long hair—dark, fair, grey, white, all dirty—overflowed the sacks and newspapers and torn overcoats: white faces leered, eyes semi-sealed with crusty scum or blank behind their closed lids. The air was thick and heavy. In the street above, traffic moved; hurrying footsteps boomed on the wood of the pavement-set cover, and through the cracks water dripped: a rainy day.

Shard sat up, head aching: the meths and the atmosphere had combined cruelly. He looked around more closely from his new position. His right-hand neighbour was a woman: naked breasts flopped sideways free of newsprint, a nipple overshadowing a picture of Edward Heath in *The Sunday Telegraph*. The breasts were thinly flaccid and the face gaunt and yellow, yet Shard believed the woman to be young, at least in years. He recoiled in horror: people like these he had met often enough in his days as an ordinary copper in the Metro, but he had not lived with them, woken up in the early morning with them, so close as to feel their cold-sweating flesh against his own.

He saw a man watching him from a corner, a man who seemed tall as he lay beneath an overcoat, booted feet projecting into freedom.

The admitting man, hall-porter of the night before?

Right! The man spoke: Shard fancied the accent was East Anglian. 'Sleep well, mate?'

'Yes, thanks.'

'Jesus, I'm dry.'

'What d'you drink?'

A hoarse laugh, scornful: 'Christ! Any bloody thing.'

Shard got to his feet, picked his way over and between the dead-out bodies, bringing out the meths bottle. Reaching the tall man, he took a

55

grip on his guts and swigged—just a little for local colour: one thing sure, he didn't want to put his lips to the rim after the tall man. Then he handed the bottle over.

'Thanks, mate.' The tall man drank, left just a little behind. The tongue came out, licking around the lips, not wasting a drop that could be gathered in by a little effort. 'Where you from, then?'

'London.'

'The Smoke, eh. How d'you come up—motorail?'

Shard grinned. 'Yes, with the Rolls. Jeeves is getting on in years, for long drives.'

A fit of coughing, night-suspended, started: the tall man went from white to purple, nearly strangling. 'Wet bloody day, tickles me bloody tubes.' Cough, cough, cough—then violent ejection, past Shard, glutinous, horrible. 'Sorry, mate.'

'And you?'

'Me?'

'Where from? Been here long, in York?'

'Long enough. Go back south if I had the bloody strength left. Too bloody cold up here, too bloody wet, too much bloody fog. What you want to come for?'

Shard shrugged. 'Change of air.' Time might be short and getting shorter, but it was always a mistake to rush things.

Cough, cough. 'Done any bird, have you?'

The tall man paused. 'Don't be shy in this house. *I*'ve done bird.' Haunted eyes examined Shard. 'You don't have the look, quite...'

'What look?'

'On the road look, or the dropout look. You can tell. So I reckon it's a case of bird—see?'

Shard laughed. 'Okay, you're right. The Ville—three years. GBH.'

'The Ville, eh.'

'That's right. Though I got picked up in Ireland, Dublin.'

'Dublin, eh.'

'That's right.' Shard laughed again. 'So now I aim to start life afresh.'

★   ★   ★

Hesseltine was on the phone, early that morning, to Hedge at home, Hedge shaving soft pink skin. 'What is it?' Hedge snapped down the line when summoned from his bathroom.

'Hedge, have you any word from Shard?'

'No! And don't expect to, yet.'

'Then you've not read the papers—'

'No, I haven't. I'm *shaving*, Hesseltine.'

'I apologise. Late last night a car crashed on the M1 just south of the M18 junction. Fatally. It was Shard's car—'

'My God—is Shard—'

'No, Hedge. The body wasn't Shard's. Enquiries have just revealed that it was a DC

from York. I thought you ought to know.'
Hesseltine paused. 'This is getting police-
depletive. I don't like that. I hope you'll pull
your finger out, Hedge.'

He rang off.

★   ★   ★

They walked, the tall man and Shard—looking
for chances, as the tall man put it, what they
might find to eat or flog. The tall man's name
was Nose: he wouldn't admit to more than that.
His nose was not big enough to account for the
nickname: it was the fact that, continually when
not coughing, he picked it, a revolting
performance. They walked wet pavements
beneath a brighter sky, a promise of a nice clear
day. Hungry, with the aroma of meths on the
breath of Nose, and on his whiskers, they
walked back beneath Monk Bar, into the walled
city, shambling along with Shard
uncomfortable and scruffy behind face stubble.
It didn't take Shard any time to pick up one
thing: they were under surveillance—or
anyway, he was. He recognised the fresh
youthful face: the DC of the night before, in a
plain car caught in the jam of traffic just inside
the gate, waiting for the lights to change against
the road from Thirsk. He saw the eyes: he had
been recognised too. The traffic began to move,
the jack disappeared behind. Farther on, as

58

Shard and Nose headed up along Goodramgate, the DC passed again, going the other way. He'd lost no time in turning, and he was talking into a two-way radio. The next move came as no surprise to Shard: two uniformed coppers, closing in from ahead to take forearms in hard grips.

Shard protested, questioned, authenticating himself in the eyes of Nose. Nose was entirely philosophic: 'It's to be expected, mate, they don't like our smell. This, it's part of tourist Britain and we spoil the bloody scenery.' Peaceably, they were led to the nick. It was an experience Shard had never undergone and one he didn't like: the crowds, all the searching eyes, the backward looks, the disdain—the fearful wonder in the eyes of children. Growing angry as he was marched along, he felt that the DC could have found a better way.

At the nick, separation: goodbye to Nose, busily picking. In the charge room with the DC, Shard jerked a hand along the direction taken by his late colleague.

'Don't take it out on him. He's harmless if filthy.'

'We won't, sir. A talking-to about the company he keeps, then he'll go on his way.'

Shard stared. 'Company he keeps? Me?'

'That's right, sir. We had word from London to pick you up. Wanted in connexion with a break-in.'

'That's what you're going to tell him?'

'Yes, sir—'

'You blow my working base without my say-so. Why?'

'We have some information, sir, and the DI thinks you may wish to act on it. The DI's on his way down. He'll tell you himself.'

Shard grunted irritably and sat himself down on a hard chair. 'In the best Barlow circles, the villain always gets the offer of a cigarette.'

'Sorry, sir.' Out came a packet.

'And a cup of tea. Only make mine coffee. And bacon and eggs. It wouldn't break the canteen kitty, would it, if you were to give that other poor bastard the same before you hoof him out?'

The DC went off: Shard sat and looked at bareness, featurelessness. Pale green walls, plain wooden table, kitchen chairs. He'd been in more such rooms than he cared to remember, and compared with the cellar of his night's lodging it was, of course, paradise: but somehow he couldn't rid himself of the feeling of being, this time, on the other side, the arrest side. It made the room look and feel different. Even the DI, coming in soon after his DC's departure for food, looked threatening. Stupid! Yet there was, undeniably, an atmosphere. The DI was tight-lipped, white. Shard stood up.

'I'm told you have something for me, Mr Gleeson?'

60

'I have.'

'Good, or not?'

'You'll have to judge that for yourself, sir.'
The voice was hard. 'Before I come to that,
there's something else. Your car—it crashed on
the motorway. My DC was killed, Mr Shard.'

Shard drew in breath, shocked, shaken. 'On
my account. God, I'm sorry.'

'So am I, sir.' The voice shook a little; there
was accusation in the air. In today's climate, the
police were always in the front line, but it was
never popular when the brass descended out of
London and pulled rank: when the bright
notions of the brass led to death in one's own
force, the reaction was strong and bitter.

Shard asked, 'Foul play, anything
deliberate?'

'No, sir, apparently not. Foul luck! A wet
road, and a skid on overtaking a container
transporter. No one's to blame, but...'

'I know. Except me ... I understand, and
again, I'm sorry.'

'Well, we'll say no more, sir. What I have to
tell you—' The DI broke off, turning as the
door opened: the DC came in with a tray of
food which he put in front of Shard. 'I'll talk
while you eat,' the DI said, and Shard nodded.
He sat down and got on with breakfast: it
descended into a stomach that didn't know it
was so meths-queasy till eggs and bacon made
their entry, after which Shard felt decidedly

61

sick. He pushed the rest away and drank black coffee, and listened. York police had definitely picked up something; it remained to be seen whether or not it was germane, but it had the initial sound of being tailored to fit at least in part: there was a word in the grapevine, a word that someone was short of a safeblower following a nasty accident to the resident expert.

'Casey?'

'Could be, Mr Shard, just could be.'

'But if Casey was to be their peterman... God, he was after more than that! London underground—it's rather bigger than a safe, isn't it?'

Gleeson shrugged. 'Might be a euphemism. They're not going to advertise openly.'

'True.' Shard lit another offered cigarette and blew smoke thoughtfully. 'It fits, I believe. Who is it that's put the word around? Dark skinned—or not?'

'We don't know the originators. Our informant's contact was white—British. That doesn't have to mean a lot.'

'No, that also is true.' Shard frowned. 'If the Middle East's involved ... they wouldn't be *au fait* with our home products, they'd need to put out feelers.'

'No substitutes lined up—that's what I reckoned, Mr Shard.' The DI paused expectantly. 'Do you play on that wicket?'

'Me, in person?'

'I'm told you know about explosives.'

'I do. In broad outline—maybe a little more than that. But I'm not, definitely not, an expert. Like Casey.'

'Any port in a storm, sir!'

'Oh, thanks very much,' Shard said sardonically. He drummed fingers on the table, absently. 'There'll be other applicants—it's a top job! What have you in York, and round about?'

'Two good petermen, Ferret Yates and Dandy O'Sullivan, known to be in the vicinity. O'Sullivan here in York, Yates in Ripon. No others known to us. But that doesn't really help much, does it, Mr Shard? The grapevine operates nation-wide.'

'Yes. How did you get your info—or shouldn't I ask?'

The DI said formally, 'One of our known snouts, sir.'

'Reliable?'

'Usually, very reliable.' Gleeson paused, then went on, 'I could always bring in Yates and O'Sullivan, just to have a word . . . helping with enquiries generally. It'd reduce the competition.'

'No.' Shard shook his head. 'You wouldn't be able to hold 'em long enough, and it would smell a little high in the circumstances.' He grinned. 'Like I do. Can you fix me a bath?'

'Shower in the washroom, sir. It's all yours. Does this mean you're batting, Mr Shard?'

Yorkshire was a cricketing county: Shard grinned to himself. He said, 'Fix me some pads and flannels and I'll go in and hit the bowling for six—I hope! Yes, I'll go in, Inspector, but I'll need to make a call to London first.'

★　　　★　　　★

'Hedge?'

There was an indeterminate sound at the London end of the security line. 'Is that Shard?'

'Yes, Hedge—'

'Heard about your car?'

'Yes. I needn't say, I'm desperately sorry about the DC—'

'Did he exist, or didn't he? You know what I mean. What do I do?' Incipient panic, a heartfelt plea for a firm decision to be made, extended along the wire.

Shard said, 'He didn't, I did. Now I'm dead. Listen, Hedge.' As concisely as he could, Shard passed on the York DI's information. Hisses and gasps smote his ear. He cut in: 'Hedge, it's the best lead I'm likely to get, and time presses—'

'My God, Shard, you don't have to tell me that—'

'Then give me, in your own best interest, your blessing.'

'Well . . .'

'Thanks, Hedge, thanks very much. Even if I don't get the job, I'll get some of the gen—bound to.'

'If they're the right people.'

'If they're not, nothing's lost—except, I agree, a little time. I'll be fast. Here's my story, Hedge, and when the check-out goes through the grapevine, I'll expect confirmation from your end. I was in the army—bomb disposal—Belfast. A big explosives expert . . . let's say, Staff-Sergeant Royal Engineers, name . . . John Pearson. Time expired, and disillusioned—with civvy street and the British in Northern Ireland both. Can't get the kind of work I want. Sickened by what the British have done—used to say so while I was still serving.' Shard developed his theme, giving Hedge time to make notes, detailing his service career.

'Have you,' Hedge asked, 'the background knowledge to cope?'

'Factually, as you should know, I did a course on explosives with the army, while I was still at the Yard, so the answer's yes, just about—hopefully. There's one other thing: I've done time for GBH, three years in Pentonville, just come out. That checks with something else—I play safe when possible. All right, Hedge?'

'I suppose so—'

'Now—Beth. My wife, Hedge. I'm going to

ask you to tell her I'm alive and never mind the news when it breaks. Will you?'

Hedge snapped, 'No. If you're dead, Shard, you're dead. You know that. No, I won't!'

'I didn't think you would,' Shard said bitterly. He rang off before he added something he might regret, and, thinking of Beth, went for a shower and a change of clothing. This was Mrs Casey all over again, in a reverse sense: he sighed as the warm soapy water cleared away the traces of the night before. Coppers' wives had much to put up with, and real widowhood was the worst possibility. At least Beth's tears would be brief, would end in happiness: Tom Casey's widow had yet to learn her state, and from that no release would ever come, any more than it would to that DC's family, which was something Shard would never cease to blame himself for, the more so as the death had resulted from a stupid and pointless whim.

★   ★   ★

Nose, duly hoofed out, met renewed rain as he left the nick: it fell upon the threadbare shoulders of his tattered and torn overcoat, which was paper-thin, first constructed in pre-war days—built to last, but not night and day. Nose picked and coughed and shambled, bereft of his short-while partner. The fuzz had been quite decent: the remains of a fag hung from Nose's lower lip, increasing his cough but bringing balm nevertheless. Breakfast had fallen from heaven, better than mere nectar. Mistake, they'd said, it was his mate they wanted to question. But he might be some help: he had been just that, telling the fuzz what little he knew about his mate, and no harm done thereby. The fuzz had made a donation: fifty pees. Very welcome!

Nose moved on, just wandering in the rain.

★   ★   ★

Detective Inspector Gleeson had said the grapevine's indication was that a middle-aged man named Larger would receive applications. Mr Larger, known both to the police and fellow villains, on account of his tastes, as Harp Lager with a hard g, could be contacted most afternoons in a newsagents' three streets away from the nick, a newsagents' that had a busy under-the-counter trade in hard porn. But it was another avenue that would provide the path to employment.

Shard, at two thirty, set foot on that path. There were two people in the shop when he entered, a young man and a woman, both porn-innocent. Shard hung about, looking furtive, till they'd gone. Then he approached the counter.

'Mr Larger?'

A nod: 'That's me.'

'Who they call—Harp Lager?'

'Aye. What do you want, then?' Mr Larger's eyes looked down meaningly.

'Just a word.'

'Not—pictures?'

'No. Not pictures. A private word. I believe you sell fireworks, Guy Fawkes time.'

'Ah ... ha! Hang on a tick.' Mr Larger turned away, opened a door behind, and leaned through. 'Ethel! Come down a moment, eh? I got some business to do.' He turned back to Shard and served a customer who had just come in. Shard waited again, wandering around the shop. After a while he found his attention caught by the window: flattened against it, with an astonished expression written big, was a filthy whiskery face wildly framed in dank rats'-tails of hair, a familiar face engaged in familiar action: pick, pick, pick. Recognition was only too obvious: as Ethel came in behind the counter, Mr Larger cottoned on to Nose.

'Friend of yours?'

'No.'

'Seems to know you...'

'Bloody scrounger.' Shard laughed. 'I gave a bloke like that a ten pence piece this morning. Could be him.'

Mr Larger came out from behind his counter, approaching the door. 'Bugger off,' he said sharply. 'I'll call the police else.' He glared: he

68

had a mean face, a dangerous face. Nose shambled off, with a backward look at Shard, who kept his face blank. Mr Larger turned and came back in and lifted the flap of the counter for Shard. 'After you,' he said. 'Right through to the back.'

Shard went through with Mr Larger behind, close. There was a strong feeling of danger now, of very burning boats. Something about Mr Larger said clearly that a sanctum was about to be penetrated, and not with impunity.

CHAPTER SIX

The room was small and dark, with cheap furniture and linoleum on the floor: below a small and dirty-paned window, the Ouse flowed. Shard was told to sit: he did so, in a creaking basket-work chair at a table covered with a multi-coloured patchwork cloth as dirty as the window panes, greasily dirty.

Larger looked at him narrowly: Larger was a short, square-bodied man with a thick neck and the shoulders of a bison. The face was also square—heavy and pasty, and the head was bald, a dangerous-looking man with a protuberant lower lip. He stood there, breathing heavily, and asked: 'Well?'

'They said apply here.'

'They?'

'Two fellas I met.'

'Where d'you meet these two fellas?'

Shard jerked his head in an encompassing geographical movement. 'Boozer. We got talking.'

'Names?'

'I didn't ask.'

'Describe them.'

Personal descriptions could be nicely generalised: Shard gave two, sounding vague. Larger didn't offer comment on them as such, but asked what had been said.

'They said someone was looking for a peterman.'

'Did they now.' Larger's gaze was steady, searching, weighing. 'That fits you?'

'Well,' Shard said, 'not quite it doesn't. That, I have to admit.'

'Then?'

'I can learn—'

'Learn!' Larger's tone was acid. 'There's plenty around who don't need to learn.'

Shard shrugged. 'Okay, okay. It was worth a try, wasn't it? You could need me sometime, even if not now. I can kind of leave my card, perhaps.'

Larger kept his eyes searching. He asked, 'Know anything about explosives?'

'Plenty. That's why I came on the chance. I was in the army.' Meaningly he added,

70

'Belfast.'

Larger nodded, slowly. 'Tell me all about it.' Shard did so, repeating all he had told Hedge on the telephone, expanding on it. Larger listened and was obviously interested in all he heard: Shard knew he had made an impression when at last Larger said, 'All right. There's some people I'd like you to meet.'

'Whatever you say. When?'

'Sooner the better. Tonight, if I can fix it. No promises, but they could be interested.'

'Thanks,' Shard said. 'And in the meantime?'

'In the meantime, you stay here.' It was pleasantly said, not far off an invitation to stay for tea, but Shard didn't doubt the score for a moment. Meantime, was the time for the check-out and if it failed to hold together then he was handily adjusted for the drop. He remained seated at the table; Larger left the room. Shard heard the tinkle of a lifted telephone: he got up and put an ear to the door, but could hear nothing. He went back to his chair and waited. Larger didn't re-appear: he was probably back behind his shop counter, selling newspapers, fags, lollies and porn. Time dragged past in a blank silence. Even the invisible telephone didn't ring. At six thirty by Shard's watch, a sound came from the shop and from it Shard judged Larger to be closing for the night. A few minutes later he was summoned to another room for tea, which he

71

took with Mr and Mrs Larger: ham-and-eggs, followed by parkin, mealy and treacly, washed down with strong tea, after which, not seeming to notice the mixture, Mr Larger opened a bottle of Harp for himself. Nobody spoke much, but Larger, when he did utter, talked about the army: it seemed he had done National Service just after the war, with a local regiment of the line. Private Larger, undistinguished infantryman: ex-Staff-Sergeant John Pearson kept his end up without difficulty—in the interval, the army had in any case changed out of all recognition. Tea finished and was cleared away by Ethel Larger. Mr Larger sat smoking a pipe.

'These people I'm to meet,' Shard said. 'When?'

'Let you know when I know myself,' Larger said, around his pipe-stem. They carried on waiting and Shard's nerves began to play him up: the waiting game he detested as much as anyone else. Larger read an evening paper, concentrating on the sporting pages, not appearing bothered about delays. Shard told himself that delay was inevitable and did not have to spell doom: it would take time for Hedge to feed enough into the pipeline to get him by—Hedge with his army-sized network of contact men, snouts, spies, agents provocateurs and what-have-you, the men who talked out of the sides of their mouths in pubs and caffs, in all the right places, listening and giving the right answers, men who were in the full confidence of the kind of people who would be doing Largers' check-out for him. It was near enough foolproof, but it took time. That night, the telephone rang twice, but Larger was non-committal after, shrugging off Shard's question. By bedtime nothing had jelled: Shard was given a shake-down in an upstairs room after a cup of cocoa and more parkin; the door was locked behind him. He looked out of the window: sheer brick sides down to the river. A dive could carry him clear, but to what? Unless the locking of the door had been no more than a useless gesture, someone would be keeping a lookout on the river below—and in any case he had his duty. The long night passed: Shard slept uneasily, too conscious of all the possible slips, of the hours passing away towards the big bang in London's underground system. In the morning the dawn's light woke him, and he lay and listened—for telephones, for the Larger's stirring. Someone was up early for the newspaper rounds and the six a.m. workers: Shard heard the creaking of the stairs and the opening and shutting of doors. At seven thirty he was brought down for breakfast by Ethel Larger, a silent meal again with Larger and his wife taking bites between summonses to the shop. Larger brought a paper in, chucked it unconcernedly at Shard, who read and tried not

73

to show interest. A Detective Chief Superintendent named Simon Shard, of the Metropolitan Police—FO cover held even after death—had been killed in an accident on the M1 motorway. Shard convinced himself hopefully that Larger was not showing undue interest in his reactions as he read. Reading, Shard thought principally of Beth.

More waiting, waiting all morning. It was once again afternoon, and later afternoon at that, when, like all things, waiting ended: Shard, in the back room again, heard the ring of the telephone, heard Ethel call for her husband. Larger was not long on the phone: the tinkle indicated the cut-off, another tinkle indicated an outgoing call, and soon after this Larger came in. His face gave nothing away but his words brought comfort: Hedge must have got through the net nicely. Larger nodded and said, 'Okay. We leave when the car gets here.'

'When's that?'

'After I shut.'

      ★   ★   ★

In London, Hedge co-ordinating in Shard's absence, the unobtrusive counter-measures were getting under way. A close watch was placed on all stations, plain-clothes details on a twenty-four hour guard; bomb-disposal teams were quietly drafted in, taking up quarters in

Wellington Barracks, together with sappers from Chatham with mine-detector equipment. Helicopters stood ready at short notice to ferry infantry into the capital from Colchester and Salisbury Plain and Aldershot, men who would be used for crowd-control or to empty and seal all stations if the word should come. The files of all London Transport underground employees were checked by officers of the Special Branch. At night in the train-free hours, plain-clothes police and army experts searched subway tunnels, stations and the 238 route miles of the track itself under an official cloak of a structural survey of possible stresses and strains likely to be brought about by a supposedly projected reconstruction of London's sewerage system. And all the time that Hedge-topped network of careful listeners kept its myriad antennae tuned to pick up any careless talk on the part of terrorism. All that could reasonably be expected at this stage, was being done: but Assistant Commissioner Hesseltine, conferring once again with Hedge, the Home Secretary and the military command, summed it up succinctly.

'If it happens, we can't prevent war-scale casualties. There's still just the one thing: close the system!'

★   ★   ★

The car took Shard out of York on the A59 for

Green Hammerton, passing on its way the road down which Casey had walked just four days previously. At Green Hammerton it left the Harrogate road and headed on the A1167 for Boroughbridge, after which, crossing over the A1, it made towards Ripon. Larger was not present: Shard had been picked up by a driver and three other men, all British apparently. He sat in the back between two of them, both armed, both refusing to answer questions. From Ripon the car headed out north–west, turning off left into Wensleydale just short of Leyburn. In Wensleydale Shard looked out at Pennine peaks, at low stone walls, sheep on the road, and a rushing river tearing over rocks, at white puffy clouds hastening over the fells: few people, and, outside the small clusters of villages, few houses. Just before Bainbridge the driver swung left, following a signpost for Stalling Busk. The road climbed steeply after a while, ascending a lonely, desolate fellside, heavenward-heading. They dropped down past Semerwater, sunset-reddened and slightly ruffled, climbed again along a narrow track of ruts and pot-holes. In the isolated village of Stalling Busk, a place of old weatherworn stone farm buildings, the car drove into a farmyard. Behind the cover of the wall and the fading daylight, Shard was brought out with a gun in his spine and ordered through a side door into the farmhouse. He smelt cow and pig, and damp straw: then the door was shut and bolted behind him.

He looked around: he was in a passage leading to a square hall. Ahead, another door opened off the passage. The house was silent, felt damp from neglect and desertion.

He asked, 'Journey's end?'

'Stopover.' The gun pressed. 'And grill. Move. Door on your right.'

Shard moved, halted by the door. A hand reached round him and shoved it open. The room was plain and bare: a table, a chair, a heavily barred window, an immensely strong door. Stone-flagged floor, thick walls of bare stone. Nothing else—just himself, and two of the men, men whom during the drive in he had come to know, unhelpfully, as Terry and Nigel. They were both young and both looked intelligent enough beneath the long hair: not physical thugs, but Shard had an instinct that told him they could be about to behave as such just the same. When Terry shut the door and locked it, pocketing the key, Shard saw something hanging on the wall behind, something revealed by the closing of the door: something of rusty iron, a circular flat band with inward-pointing iron spikes along two-thirds of its length, with one end sliding into a thumb-screw. He had seen similar objects in museums, in ancient crumbling castles whose dungeons harked horribly back to the Dark

Ages. It was big enough to belt a man's waist—or a woman's, when required. It could, he supposed, accurately be called a talking-piece.

★ ★ ★

Back in York, Larger was looking anxious, pulling at his chin and staring into the living-room's gas fire. Ethel remarked on his preoccupation.

'Worrying about Pearson?' she asked.

'Well—I don't know really. Yes, I suppose I am. It's my responsibility, you know.'

Ethel, sewing a button-hole, bit off cotton. 'Nothing's likely to go wrong, dear.'

'I don't know so much. There was a bloke, a tramp . . .'

'Oh?'

Larger explained. 'Saw him again this afternoon as a matter of fact—this evening, after the car'd left. Standing and staring at the window. Funny—or could be.'

'Why,' his wife asked, 'didn't you go out and talk to him?'

'Don't know why not,' Larger said irritably. Then he added, 'Yes, I do. I was thinking of having a word when the law come along and chivvied him away. I didn't want to have any barney with the law, did I?'

Ethel bit more cotton and went off at a

78

tangent. 'You take your tablets, did you?'

'Eh?'

'Tablets, dear—'

'Yes!' Silence: things nagged at Larger. He grew restless. After a while he banged out his pipe in a heavy brass ashtray and stood up. 'I'll go and see a pal of mine,' he said.

'About your tramp?'

Larger nodded.

'Never find him, will you? They all look alike.'

'They don't all pick their noses,' Larger said in an aggrieved tone, 'and he was tall with it. You never know . . . they tend to congregate in dosshouses. This friend of mine, you don't know him, Ethel, he picks things up what other people don't. Worth a shot in the dark . . . just to put me mind to rest like.'

He went out.

CHAPTER SEVEN

The man called Terry indicated the chair and said, 'Sit.' Shard sat. There was little daylight left now; the other man, Nigel, flicked on a light, then crossed to the barred window and yanked heavy shutters across, securing them with a metal rod.

Shard asked, 'What's the idea?'

'Questions,' Terry said. 'I thought I told you—you're here for the grill.'

Shard shrugged. 'So you did. Start grilling.'

'You don't object?'

'Why should I? I'd expect you to satisfy yourselves, just like any other prospective employer.'

Terry smiled, a smile that failed to warm the cold eyes. Those eyes were fishlike, small and pink-rimmed, and the face had an unhealthy pallor. He and his companion remained standing, with their backs to the door now. The guns were not out, but were handy in shoulder holsters. Shard knew the interrogation would be tough—that was to be expected, but there was a hard, almost feline quality in Terry's face, the callousness of the homosexual in certain situations of power, that gave Shard an extra awareness of danger. 'We'll start at the beginning,' Terry said, staring at Shard, arms folded across a thin body as he lay back against the door. 'Where and when born, names of parents, occupation of father, names of schools.'

Christ, Shard thought, but kept his face blank. This, he had not expected: it could be bluff, but if they should check it out, and they had the time to do just that, then it was all going to fall apart. In the meantime, the question hung in the air, very bad game indeed. There was only one thing to do, and Shard did it: names apart, he told the truth: this had the advantage that he wouldn't, at least, trip over his own tongue. The information was absorbed into a tape recorder produced by Nigel. The questions proceeded towards Shard's career in the army: he gave the answers he had already passed to Hedge. He was closely questioned about Belfast; this was easy, since he had once worked on a job in Northern Ireland in co-operation with the military authorities and the RUC. His political views and alignments were sought and digested into the tape. He had views but no positive alignments: the views he gave were naturally phoney, tailored to fit requirements. He could only hope they would withstand the further check, that Hedge had pulled his finger out and used his imagination as to whom he primed. The army led to civil life and Pentonville and the GBH that had put him there, and Shard kept his story straight, repeating what he had already told Larger back in York. Shard had done well—he knew that: the eyes had grown friendlier in the two searching faces, the horrible instrument hanging from its hook on the wall began to lose its immediacy. But it all depended on the check: basically, it was a simple question of time.

The questions became technical: what did ex-Staff-Sergeant Pearson know of the handling of explosives?

'Enough.'

'To handle safely and intelligently . . . what?'

'Dynamite, TNT, jelly . . . you name it, I've met it.'

Once again, glances were exchanged, a look this time of faint amusement. 'This is bigger, boyo! This is nuclear.'

★ ★ ★

Casually said: Shard had caught his breath. Casey had said it was to be big; but there were degrees of bigness and Shard had never imagined this, though, knowing it now, he saw the logic. It was a known fact that some at least of the various terrorist organisations had gained access to things nuclear; the first of Heathrow's military encirclements some while ago had been due to knowledge that some ground-to-air missiles had passed into the wrong hands.

He had failed to conceal shock.

'Surprised, eh?'

'You might say so. Look, what's in the air? Can I ask that now?'

Terry shook his head. 'Not yet. There'll come a time when you'll have to be told. For now, patience.' He paused, eyes searching Shard's face again. 'Can you handle nuclear explosive?'

'I think,' Shard said, glad and sorry at the same time for divers reasons, 'that I'll have to say—no. That is, I've absorbed some of the theory ... and I'm familiar with nuclear warheads in missiles ... that sort of thing. I've no experience of rendering safe or anything like that. That didn't come into the day's work ... not when I was in Belfast.'

Terry rubbed at his chin. 'That won't matter, not really. It's basic experience of siting explosives that we need, siting them where they're wanted in spite of ... difficulties. And seeing to it that they give their full potential—you know, proper tamping and that, packing 'em down hard so they don't waste their force on the fresh air. I'm talking as a non-professional, but you'll know what I mean.'

Shard nodded. 'Yes, I know what you mean. You don't want me actually to prepare the charges?'

'No. They're prepared already, no worries there.'

★   ★   ★

A camp bed was brought in and Shard was left alone behind the lock and the bolts and the bars. Outside, a rising wind whistled over the fells and soon Shard heard a patter of rain blown against the window outside the shutter. As the wind increased, even the thick walls of the old farmhouse seemed to shake: the rusty iron device on the stone vibrated, at least in

83

Shard's imagination, as though preparing its wicked teeth to bite human flesh . . . Shard gave an involuntary shiver, thinking of the further check that had no doubt already started: on the way in he had seen the telephone wires, the skeletonic line of poles bringing communication along beside the muddy track from the main A684 to the village of Stalling Busk, lost in the rain and mists of the Pennines. *What was to happen to London?* London had just six days left—his watch said one thirty-three and the date was April 28th—six days to an appalling subterranean tragedy if the date remained unaltered: and he had a feeling that this was so. His questioner, growing talkative after a meal and a thermos of coffee, had confirmed Tom Casey's death as being nothing directly to do with the job in hand: Casey, it seemed, was not known to have been in contact with Shard. Shard chalked up a credit for himself: Casey's death had indeed been a *crime passionel*. According to these men, the woman in the top job, still no names mentioned, had given Shard's predecessor his opportunity and it had been taken: the woman's lover had been unhappy.

'Hence me?' Shard, all innocence, had asked.

'Hence you. Take the tip, boyo!'

'Lay off, h'm?'

'*Right* off. She's sexy but bespoke—or kind of.' Terry didn't go into the details of how

84

revenge had been exacted: Shard was glad not to suffer a repeat—he'd seen Tom Casey, the sewn lips holding in what should never have been there, and the horrible gape between the thighs. At least he was not currently in the presence of the killer, but might yet meet him face to face, and could only trust to the self-discipline instilled by his police training. Before leaving him alone in his bare prison-bedroom, Terry had said they would be heading for HQ before the light was up, but someone else had to show first. That someone might well be Nadia Nazarrazeen, Shard fancied—or, if not, she would be at HQ.

Not long now.

★   ★   ★

A time-bomb named Larger had walked the streets of York a little earlier, directed out through Monk Bar by the knowing pal he had been to see. He found the wooden cellar-cover set in the pavement, banged, climbed the adjacent stone steps, and banged again, this time on the door of the tall, decrepit house. After a while the door was opened up.

A ragged man looked out. 'Yer?'

'Looking for someone,' Larger said. 'I'm told he's here.'

''Oo?'

'Bloke they call Nose.'

85

'Oh, yer, Nose.'

'Know him, do you?'

'Oh, yer, I know Nose.'

Larger shone a torch past the ragged man. The torch beamed into the hall, showed filth and cobwebs, met the stink on its way out to turn Larger's stomach. Larger brought out a handkerchief and held it to his face, tried not to breathe in. 'Here—is he?'

'No.'

'No?' Larger grew belligerent. 'Told he was ... I said, didn't I? Look—'

'Yer, 'e *was*. That's right.' There was a movement of a tattered arm and of fingers, and a revolting sound. The fingers blocked one nostril, the other was cleared by a mighty gale. Larger shifted sideways.

'Do you bloody *mind*?'

'Pardon. 'E's gone. Nose.'

'Christ. Where?'

The ragged man shrugged. 'Dunno. Took off late this afternoon. If asked like, I'd say 'e went south. Talked a lot about the south 'e did, London and the south.' The man sniffed, nostril nicely clear. 'Warmer like. Mind, 'e'll take it in stages.'

'First stop where?'

'Depends ... depends which way 'e's going, don't it? Could be anywhere, just anywhere.'

'Give me some addresses,' Larger said. 'Up to what ... ten miles out of York, all round.'

The ragged man obliged; Larger made notes in biro. He enquired about recent arrivals: there had been too many for the ragged man's recollection of personal details but, and this for sure, there had been none with what you might call respectable clothes. Cursing, Larger beat an angry retreat. The smallest risk was unacceptable and the bosses would crucify him if he had erred, if he had been less than thorough ... therefore, though the whole of this might well prove to be an unnecessary expenditure of time, he must find Nose somehow.

★   ★   ★

The key turned in the lock and the bolts were withdrawn. Shard, woken already by the sound, however stealthy, of a vehicle drawing into the lee of the farmyard wall, sat up in the camp bed. A voice, before the light went on, said, 'Wakey, wakey. Four a.m., time to move out. Breakfast on the move.' Terry. The light went on; Shard, stubbly himself again, stared at more stubble. From behind Terry's hair and jeans, came something on the air: pervasive, heady, sexy perfume—the top woman? The scent seemed somehow to fit the name, Nadia Nazarrazeen, nationality uncertain as yet, intentions diabolic.

He lifted an eyebrow and tapped a finger

against his nose: the response was a nod. The words, however, were workaday ones: 'Get dressed. Make it fast.'

Shard obeyed, pulling on shirt and trousers over his pants. No washing water—he hated facing any day feeling scummy and ex-bed. He thought of home, of Beth—wondered when the DC's funeral was to be and how Hedge would manage to fix *that*. There would be eventual involvements with two sets of ecclesiastical authorities if that poor DC had happened to be a Roman Catholic like Tom Casey ... and in the meantime the woman spreading stimulation outside his room was at least morally responsible in his book for too many killings already of innocents, both British and Irish. Shard, dressed, went out of the room and there she was, very Arab, immensely striking, immensely beautiful, had to be Nadia Nazarrazeen but still no names spoken so Shard had to be immensely careful...

She had brilliant dark eyes, now staring right into Simon Shard, Detective Chief Superintendent, because of his appointment to Hedge's side a very top copper. Knowing it didn't show, he prayed just the same. Her voice was clear and spoke beautiful English with only a trace of an accent: 'This is the man?'

Terry said, 'Yes.'

'He is safe?'

'I think so. There's still things for

checking—but I reckon he's all right. In any case . . . he doesn't know anything yet.'

That, Shard said to himself, is what you think. He smiled at the girl—she was little more, he fancied, just about out of her teens, but she must have broken more hearts than Casey's already. They matured fast along the Mediterranean, along the Red Sea, the Gulf, the Arabian Sea. This one looked fully experienced. Remembering Casey, Shard made the smile cautious, a mere politeness. He said, 'That's right, what the man says. Me, I'd like to know more.'

'As soon as possible, Mr Pearson.' She smiled back, an approving smile that let the even white teeth show briefly against red lips. She liked the well-built look, the shoulders, the thighs, all muscle and no fat, the flat, well-kept stomach, the chin and mouth: he could read all that in her dark eyes flanked by thick dark hair that tumbled with the world's most natural-looking artifice down the satin-smooth cheeks, palely brown in the electric light. For a moment Beth's image flashed before his mind like a warning ghost: this woman, this girl, was bloody lovely and in no time at all could slide snake-like beneath the toughest copper's skin. Beth, however was not the only warning: from behind Nadia Nazarrazeen a man came, also of the Middle East though not Shard's image of an Arab: there was none of the hauteur or the

89

dignity, none of the hawkish face and the hooked nose, no soupçon here of the flashing scimitar's blade. This man, though young, was short and all flesh, with a puffy hairless face. Probably strong though, and currently with a lover's possessive snarl in his eyes. Definitely, however passionate, unworthy of Nadia. Casey's killer? Probably: Shard marked him indelibly in his mental book.

The man put himself squatly between Shard and his Eastern beauty. 'Come,' he said in English. 'Before the light, we must go. Yes?' He looked at Nadia, and she nodded, but—curiously—her face was scornful. She moved for the door into the farmyard, out to the smell of cow and pig. Every movement of the body was sex, was a loud invitation. Dressed as an English girl she wore tight jeans, moulded to all the crevices. Shard, feeling her in his very bloodstream, watched the caressment of buttocks, one against the other. She vanished, and along the slipstream of her perfume, Shard was herded by Terry and Nigel and the squat lover, who looked as though he could be of Levantine extraction.

In the yard, still under the night's cover and the rain, stood a Dormobile—an Austin Motor Caravan, off-white with a darker stripe whose true colour only daylight would show. Nadia Nazarrazeen was already embarked, sitting on one of the passenger seats with curtains drawn across the side windows. The squat Levantine, query, sat himself fatly by her side. Shard was told to take a seat level with these two across the gangway; and by him sat Terry, with Nigel taking the front passenger seat. Already in the driving seat sat the driver: a thin man with a bilious complexion wearing a brown anorak zipped up the front to the neck and with the hood in place, giving him, from the rear, the appearance of a monk. With the farmhouse door shut and locked behind them, and the car in which Shard had been brought a few hours earlier driving out behind in the care of the third man from York, the Dormobile headed away from Stalling Busk, taking Shard once again along the rutted track past Semerwater, dark and ghostly, and on for the A684 that ran through from the A19 to Kendal in Westmorland. Reaching the main road, the Dormobile turned left, heading for the small market town of Hawes. On the outskirts of Hawes they turned off right along a road that, after two more turns, began to climb steeply into the fells above Cotterdale, heading for the Buttertubs Pass. The sky was lightening now, but there was a good deal of mist around, damply clinging, so thick at times that the beams of the headlights themselves seemed lost in it. On a bend in the high mountain road where the wreathing mist concealed a steep drop into the dale on their right, Nadia

91

Nazarrazeen, who had been preoccupied and silent since leaving Stalling Busk, spoke sharply to the driver.

'These are the Buttertubs. Stop now.'

The Dormobile, moving slow on a tricky road, eased its speed further. The headlights showed a shallow pull-in to the left, and light fencing with springy turf beyond. The driver pulled in and stopped alongside the fence.

'The lights off.'

The driver flicked a switch, and turned in his seat. For a moment there was silence. The atmosphere was curiously tense: Shard, feeling this strongly, could not have said quite why, nor could he have forecast what was about to happen. In that fraction of suspended time, that time of silence, Nadia Nazarrazeen stared ahead through the mist-blocked windscreen while the others waited for her to speak—to issue, no doubt, her further orders. No one, Shard believed afterwards, saw her hand move. But when the extraordinary silence had lasted for perhaps thirty seconds, the man by her side, the lover from the Levant, gave a brief moaning sigh and then slid into the space between the seats as limp as a discarded pair of nylon tights, with blood spreading through his shirt, messily visible as the heavy jersey rode up his body.

Then the girl spoke, calm and remote as the shrouded fells behind the mist: 'The blood—stop the flow and clean the spillage.

Undress him, bundle the clothing, and stow it out of sight. All of it. We shall get rid of that later. When he is completely naked, take him outside, but be careful with the bleeding.'

Even Terry and Nigel, so controlled and dangerous as interrogators, seemed rocked: their faces pale, they did as bid. The fawn-coloured Levantine, stripped naked, had even less dignity than before. In his left side Shard saw the tiny slit where the knife had slipped in, just right for the heart, between two ribs. Nigel dabbed with the tail of the Levantine's shirt; to Nadia Nazarrazeen's orders, Terry plugged the wound itself with one of the removed socks. Then rough bandaging was wound round and pulled tight, the rear doors were thrust open, and Terry got down. Inside the Dormobile Nigel and the driver lifted the Levantine towards the rear, and he was carried out. Nadia spoke to Shard.

'You have heard of the Buttertubs, Mr Pearson?'

Shard nodded. 'I've seen them.' Curious, he thought, what the forces of nature could accomplish over millions of years: erosion had formed the Buttertubs, deep but narrow limestone shafts that had driven into the high fell in the dawn of pre-history. 'Do I take it your late friend is going down one of them?'

'Yes.' She examined her finger-nails in the increasing, mist-filled dawn. 'He will of course be found eventually, but not in time for it to matter to me.' She wound down the window alongside her seat, and called to the men, passing the final disposal orders; then she turned back to Shard. 'A warning, my friend: that man was stupid. Because he was jealous, he killed a man who was valuable to—what I have to do.'

'Which is?'

The girl smiled. 'Patience! One lesson at a time is enough. May I suggest you learn this present one well? I am not to be trifled with, John Pearson.'

Shard sat in silence as the men got back in and checked the interior for the smallest signs of blood. The Levantine's clothing, bundled up neatly and cleanly, was pushed into the cupboard at the Dormobile's off-side rear corner. There was one thing sure: Casey's killer, now lying broken on the rocks at the bottom of one of those time-worn limestone shafts, was way beyond arrest. But the girl was still the moral killer, with as much blood on her slim, elegant fingers as had the wretched Levantine on his. As the Dormobile pulled away from deep-down death, back on the road into Muker and Swaledale, Shard was bidden to take the dead man's place beside Nadia Nazarrazeen. He obeyed, his body rigidly half-expectant of the killing knife: it was a weird feeling! From the corner of his eye he studied the face, the high cheekbones, the patrician nose, the mouth's sexy line, the tumbling dark hair. Tom Casey, poor Tom Casey, had been rather less than a good copper to allow himself to dilute duty with sex: but—and quite apart from his own built-in predilection for good-looking women—he may have had no option: sex could be considered, in the circumstances, to be duty! A copper had to convince, after all. And Nadia Nazarrazeen could be something of a man-eater.

★   ★   ★

Mile after mile, taken slow at first on the tricky, descending road, mist-shrouded still, the long drops invisible but very present. Mile after mile of sitting close up against the girl, smelling her scent, smelling her hair. She didn't utter a word: she just sat with her pointed chin cupped in a soft brown-skinned hand—just sat, and disturbed Shard—looking out of the window as later the sun came up to dapple the dales with light and life and colour. After a long, long silence, Shard risked her displeasure by asking, 'Where are we going?'

A shrug, a smile from eyes briefly slanted in his direction. 'Oh . . . a long way.'

'Tell me?'

She laughed, lightly. 'Very well, why not? To London.'

'London?' Shard felt the increased beat of his heart.

'We have finished in the north.'

'Then things are moving ... towards a conclusion?'

'There is always,' the girl said with a mocking glint in her eye, 'movement in that direction, from the start. Is this not so?'

'Yes,' Shard said. The girl seemed disinclined for more talk as the Dormobile, beginning to leave the mist behind, joined the A1. They by-passed Boroughbridge, heading towards Wetherby and on for the motorway. Shard sat wrapped in her scent, feeling the close intimacy of her body, the pressure of her thigh against his own. Her hair, taken by the wind coming through the wound-down window, blew silkily against his face. She was totally relaxed and seemed to be enjoying the drive: Shard wondered what pleasure such a girl got from killing, from the planning of mass death, all in the name, presumably, of some all-important national image, some deep-seated insane desire to impress the Western world with the latent power of her own country, whichever that might be. There had still been no suggestion of any more positive aim, of anything concrete to be gained by threat; Shard was more than ever certain that there was no blackmail of authority involved in this: it was to be mass slaughter of the most pointless kind, slaughter simply to terrify, to weaken the confidence and security of the West, as he'd said to the Garda chief in Dublin.

The Dormobile made the journey south in good time; stopping only for petrol, eating snacks on the move, they hit the end of the motorway at three thirty in the afternoon and headed along the North Circular for Gunnersbury and Kew Bridge and thence down into Twickenham. In Twickenham they pulled into a yard littered with odds and ends, a scrap-dealer's yard behind high brick walls. As the Dormobile stopped, a man with a cigarette dangling from thin lips came out from the back door of a house adjoining the yard, nodded casually at the driver, and went to shut the gate, dropping a heavy iron bar across after. Then he approached the driver's window.

'Good run, eh?'

'Very good. All okay this end?'

There was a slight pause, barely noticeable. 'Yes. All okay.' Just for a moment, eyes stared at Shard: a brief flash, maybe of no more than curiosity, but Shard for some reason didn't like it—didn't like it any more than he'd liked that so-brief pause. Beside him, the girl moved, and he got up to let her out. He came out last but one, the driver behind him. There were no guns visible as the driver put a hand on his shoulder and guided him in a friendly way towards the back door, following in the girl's scented wake:

97

but to Shard's highly tuned mind atmosphere was emerging in waves from the thin-lipped man. Ahead of him he saw the thin-lipped man whisper into the girl's ear, saw her give him a quick, sharp look, then nod. Nadia turned to face the others. 'The cellar,' she said. 'There is whisky. I shall come down in a moment.'

She went ahead with the thin-lipped man, vanishing through a door. Shard was ushered to another door which when pushed open revealed wooden steps: a light went on below, in a clean dry cellar. Shard descended. The place was littered with unmarked packing-cases, and on a plain deal table were maps and drawings which Terry and Nigel, going down ahead of Shard, gathered up into a large cardboard file and put out of sight: the new recruit, evidently, wasn't going to see the work-out yet. Across one corner of the cellar was a bar, the shelves behind it holding a number of bottles of Scotch but little else. Two of the men threw themselves into easy chairs, yawning, stretching away the cooped-up miles of motorway, calling for whisky: Nigel it was who went behind the bar to act as barman. He cocked an eye at Shard. 'Scotch?'

'Thank you.' Shard moved towards the bar.

Nigel poured, was about to shout at the others to come and get it when the door at the head of the stairs opened and Nadia Nazarrazeen came down with the thin-lipped man. Both had their guns out, and both were pointing them meaningly at Shard, who knew now that he had been dead right earlier about atmosphere. He remained standing by the bar, staring at the girl, leaving it to her to speak. She didn't keep him waiting long.

'John Pearson,' she said in a soft voice.

'Yes...'

'Who are you, John Pearson? Tell me!'

He was aware of all the eyes, like animals, waiting with claws out to rip and tear. He asked, 'Why the enquiry? Why do you doubt me?'

She was at the bottom of the steps now. 'A man, a dropout, has been found in a dosshouse south of York. They call him Nose. You know him?'

Shard nodded, feeling cold. This, he could not deny. 'I know him. So?'

'So you went to Larger's shop ... from the police station, John Pearson. What does this mean, please?'

The eyes seemed to close in: the seated men got to their feet, brought out the support guns. But they held off, waiting for word from the summit. Shard said, sounding casual, 'Oh, that's easy enough. They'd picked me up with Nose—hauled us both in, off the street.'

'Why?'

'A question about a job done down this way—a break-in, a screwing job. I had a record,

99

you see. In the copper mind, that tends to click out an answer.'

'But they let you go, John Pearson?'

He said, 'I hadn't done it, had I?'

The guns pointed still, all of them; but there was still a little time for talking. The girl asked, 'And Nose? He had done nothing either?'

'That's right. They only picked him up because he was with me when they found me.'

'And they let him go too—'

'Yes.'

'But differently.'

Shard lifted an eyebrow. 'Come again?'

The gun jerked. 'I said, but differently. Nose left the police with his filthy clothes, you did not. When you were picked up—and do not try to deny this—you were dressed like this Nose. When you went to the newsagents, you were not. Tell me, John Pearson: do the police hand out clean clothing to people accused of crime, if they are found not to have done these crimes? Is this a part of your national welfare, John Pearson?' Nadia Nazarrazeen's eyes narrowed killer-like. 'Or can there be, perhaps, John Pearson, some other reason for your fresh clothing?'

It was, he knew, all over: Beth's widowhood was now going to be for real. That, he read unmistakably in the girl's brilliant eyes. He saw the same message, repeated in the other faces, the differing facets of fear, fury, outrage, revenge and hatred. Nadia also seemed to read those faces, and she reacted sharply. 'Do not shoot,' she said. 'He can't get away. Put away your guns, all of you.'

They stared, began a reluctant back-down accompanied by protest: 'Look, he's—'

'Do as I say. Put your guns right away in case of—accidents. John Pearson will have things to tell us, and he is not to die before he has done so. Now!'

The guns went back into holsters. Shard, keeping his end up, still hoping against all reason, leant back against the bar. From the corner of his eye, as the girl moved towards him, beautiful, sexy and lethal, he saw the open bottle of Scotch. He moved fast, very fast, and with a total lack of gallantry: Johnny Walker flew strong through the air and took the girl hard in the mouth, and Shard was right behind it with one hand taking the gun in an iron grip and the other going where the bottle had landed but right around the head too, slewing the girl to place her neatly between himself and the ring of guns.

CHAPTER EIGHT

Shard held the gun against the girl's body, right between the shoulder blades. With her hair soft against his face, he gave his orders.

'Over to the wall, that side.' He gestured left of the bar. 'Move!'

They moved, taking it slow, eyes on Shard.

'Turn round, faces to the wall.'

They obeyed: the girl, who had struggled at first, was quiet and motionless in Shard's encircling grip, breathing fast, a snake in his bosom all ready to take advantage of the smallest slip. Shard called towards the line of backs. 'With great care, gentlemen, and one at a time, bring out your guns and throw them behind you. Man nearest the bar first. Go!'

They did so: weapons clattered singly on the cellar floor. Only one man, Terry, third in line, made a bid towards heroism. His gun didn't come out spinning, it came out pointing, but it never fired. Shard's bullet ripped the thumb away at the joint and went on to score a furrow along a rib and then embedded in the wall. Blood and strong language flowed: a point had been made and a broad hint taken. There was no more trouble as Shard pushed the girl ahead of him, away from the bar, along the cellar behind the silent line of rumps, towards the wooden stairway. He paused *en route* to pick up the cast guns: revolvers, automatics, quite an armoury. Stuffed as to pockets and trousers waistband, feeling like an arsenal, he reached the stairs and started up backwards, dragging his hostage and keeping wary eyes on the line of disarmed men below. They stayed like statues: he was known, now, to be a dangerous shot. Presumably they were also respecting the threat to Nadia Nazarrazeen, for they stayed like statues even after Shard had reached the top of the stairs and was emerging into the passage. It looked very much like an almost bloodless battle due to end in total victory: a flick of the door lock, then contact with a telephone to bring Hesseltine's heavies down to Twickenham and a nice easy pick-up, sunshine all the way. But it didn't come out quite like that. At the top of the steps, just before she passed out of salvation's reach, Nadia Nazarrazeen reacted twice, fast and vicious: pearly small teeth that felt diamond pointed sank deep in Shard's gun wrist, and at the same instant of time a swivelling and forcefully up-jerked knee took him very, very hard in his tenderest part. As he doubled up, the girl went down the steps like lightning. Behind her went two of the captured guns, bouncing and spinning, having exited from Shard's waistband when he fell. Using his will-power, Shard set his teeth and hinged his body upright: sweat streamed as he jerked the cellar door shut and locked it—just before a heavy man thudded against the panels. Shard heard the resulting curse, then jumped aside as bullets tore through the wood. The lock, as he had seen, was not brilliant: it wouldn't hold out for long, in fact it

103

was already splintering away.

There was only the one thing to do, and Shard did it, fast.

★   ★   ★

When safely away, he explained to Hedge: not—since he was officially dead—in his own office, or within the stately halls of the Foreign Office; but sitting on a pigeon-spotted bench on the Embankment, not far from the four old ships composing London's river navy.

'No alternative, Hedge. Absolutely none. What, I ask you, would have been the point of staying long enough to get killed?'

'I take your point,' Hedge answered, sounding stiff and unfriendly, 'but really—!'

'But really what, Hedge?'

Hedge's eyes slanted sideways. 'I beg your pardon?'

'You sound displeased,' Shard said. 'I suppose—in the Foreign Office—deadness *is* a virtue, but—'

'My dear Shard—'

'All right, all right! Just don't go on wishing me dead, that's all. I did what I could. I have addresses, I have faces.'

'What else have you?'

Shard expelled breath. 'Damn all.'

'Quite!' Hedge smiled, and it was sheer ice. '*Damn all!* Names? No?'

'One,' Shard said, 'for sure. Larger, up in York, newsagent—I told you. And almost certainly Nazarrazeen.'

'But no others?'

'First names apart—no!'

Hedge smirked. 'And the addresses—oh, a *fat* lot of use! Evacuation, obliteration—that will be the order of the day as of now ... won't it, Shard?'

'I forbear to answer questions you know the answers to, Hedge.'

'I call that impertinence, Shard.'

'So do I, Hedge. It was meant to be. How long does this go on?'

Hedge stared. 'How long does what go on?'

'The slanging match—Foreign Office style, of course, we're not common coppers. I think we're wasting precious time. You realise there's just five days to go now? Maybe less—since this time they'll know for sure something's leaked!' Shard cocked an eye at Hedge, looking sardonic. 'You did take it in, I suppose, when I said it's nuclear?'

'Of course I did!'

'I'm glad. I've found it galvanic news.'

'What's that supposed to mean?'

'It's galvanised me back to life, Hedge—'

'Oh, no, it hasn't! You're dead. Dead you stay! I've gone to immense trouble—'

'I'm sorry, Hedge, trouble or not, I'm coming alive again as of this very minute—'

'But damn it all, Shard, the funeral's tomorrow!' Hedge fumed, eyes starting from a face of deepest pink, umbrella waving like a regimental colour, the Whitehall regimental colour. 'The whole thing's been arranged—'

'Then disarrange. Look *I* wasn't going physically into that coffin in any case, was I? You have a body, and I'm sorry to say it, very sorry. That DC won't be sailing under false colours after all, and that's all there is to it. Me, I'm back in circulation, all ready to co-ordinate again, but first I'm going home to see my wife—'

'But a dead man—'

Shard swivelled on the bench, thrust his face into that of Hedge and spoke with quietly insistent belligerence. 'Listen, Hedge. I'm back alive. My death's been overtaken by events and isn't necessary any more. The other side, the villains—they *know* we're on to them now. I agree that's bloody unfortunate, but it's also a bloody *fact*. In the meantime, there may be some news from Assistant Commissioner Hesseltine.'

'Why Hesseltine?'

Shard said, 'I made contact soonest possible after I got away. Too late for the villains to be netted, of course, but there could be traces left.'

Hedge looked apoplectic. 'You contacted Hesseltine—before myself, Shard?'

'Yes. Case of speed. There's something about

106

the Yard . . . they tick over faster when a dead man comes on the blower, Hedge. Faster than the FO. By the way, I'd suggest you put wheels in motion about that DC from York—he'll have parents, Hedge. If you're half-way human, you'll postpone the funeral till they've adjusted.'

★   ★   ★

When Shard reached his home in Ealing, he was met by the half-expected though unhoped-for: Mrs Micklam, short, thick and fussy. She made him feel what he was supposed to be: death. He managed a smile and said, 'Hullo, mother-in-law, you needn't look so . . . surprised.' He had been about to say, so disappointed; but had realised the cruelty to Beth. 'After all, I *am* a policeman.'

Mrs Micklam, for once wordless, had fallen back against the wall, just inside the front door, shaking her head from side to side and staring. She might have been looking at a ghost: in case she thought she was, Shard reached out, laid a hand on her arm, gently.

'Beth?' he asked. 'Where is she?'

Mrs Micklam cried, tears coursing down pale yellow cheeks. 'Simon, you might have phoned first.'

'I did. There was no reply.'

'Oh . . . yes. We've been out. I thought it

107

better for my poor child . . . than just sitting.'

He nodded. 'Where is she?'

'The drawing-room.'

He removed his hand from her arm. 'Leave us alone, mother-in-law.' He moved down the hall, opened the door, looked in: she was sitting on the floor in front of the gas fire, face white and far away, clothes looking as if they'd been dragged on, an old jersey and a skirt that should have gone to a jumble sale years ago. She had the photograph albums out, crucifying herself. He coughed. He said, 'Beth,' and held out his arms to her.

She looked up, eyes wide.

'Darling, it's all right. It's me. I'm back, safe and sound. They couldn't tell you. I'm so desperately sorry, but it's all over now.'

★ ★ ★

Shard headed later for Grosvenor Square and the US Embassy, where he had good contacts; certain items he had read in recent months, not all of them especially classified, led him to suppose that Embassy files on the American nuclear programme might be worth study: he found they were. Leaving the Embassy for Seddon's Way via underground from Bond Street, he automatically watched the evening crowds on the platform and in the train with half his attention: while there was nothing very

108

specific to watch out for, other than known faces who were unlikely to show themselves, there was always the chance and no copper could neglect it. But his thoughts were seething around un-policemanlike matters: the job was a bastard, was destructive of home life, of domestic happiness. Beth, in the grip of a wicked reaction, had thrown it all in his face: Hedge, the constant late hours, the separations, the uncertainties, the impossibilities of making any sort of off-duty arrangements when off-duty virtually did not exist. The constant worrying over the years as to what might have happened to him ... culminating in preparations for his funeral. Flowers, graves ... the Yard—not, of course, Hedge's outfit—had been making all the actual committal arrangements, but naturally she had been involved. She had not—and now she knew why—been permitted to see the body: there had been hints of terrible injuries, left mostly in the air by Assistant Commissioner Hesseltine whom never, but never, would she have inside the house again. Mrs Micklam, later, had summed it all up concisely: diabolical cruelty, she said, wicked and incredible. If he had any feeling at all for his wife, he would resign at once. At that, he had merely shrugged and turned away. Mrs Micklam's voice had rattled around him, beating off the walls till he had turned again and in a voice of cold steel told her to shut up or be thrown out. She had shut up in mid sentence, yellow skin shrivelling, face crumpling. His words had brought quiet but no peace: a row with Beth had followed, and he had left for the US Embassy with the row unresolved, to hang around him in the air, something to be faced again later, something that could so easily fester under the voluble tongue of Mrs Micklam.

He rose from the tube's depths at Leicester Square and walked through to Seddon's Way off the Charing Cross Road, thoughts of mother-in-law still beating non-angelic wings in his head. A bus, as he crossed the road, avoided the reinstatement of funeral proceedings by a wheel's breadth, thus forcing his thoughts self-preservatively away from Mrs Micklam as he endured a stream of cutting comment from the scared bus driver. If mother-in-law only knew, she might be one of the thousands of victims inside the next five days, nuclearised into gas—talking gas?—as she went about her daily occasions with her shopping-basket. Hot air and Mrs Micklam: Shard made a huge effort and thought, without much benefit, of Hedge instead. In Seddon's Way he climbed the rickety, sleazy, threadbare stairs to his second floor office, which was immediately and often noisily and creakily below an establishment used for the nefarious purposes of prostitution, a wholly laughable crime in Shard's eyes and one that the police should not be expected to waste valuable time on when there was real danger elsewhere. He let himself into his office and his eyes met stamps: old stamps, new stamps on neatly mapping-penned squared sheets, British, Colonial, Foreign ... commemoratives, ordinary issues, Postage Dues, you name it. Shard had it or would get it for you at a price. When a man worked for Hedge, that man, like Hedge himself, had to have cover, and Shard officially was a commercial philatelist. In fact, good cover, papering over a multitude of activities and journeys long and short, and absences from Seddon's Way that did not have otherwise to be explained to inquisitively-matey fellow-tenants. Shard slammed the door behind him, crossed the room and brought a bottle of Scotch from a wall cupboard. He poured himself a stiff one, shot some soda in, and drank, listening to a rhythmic creak from the room above. The creak gave him bitter ideas about Mrs Micklam: a pity the White Slave trade was so fastidious! If she could be flogged off as an ancillary to the harem of some impecunious Arab who couldn't afford better ... the thought of Arabs jerked his mind back to work, and at that moment, as if in sympathy, the security line burred at him, softly, insidiously. There was no peace anywhere.

He took up the handset. 'Shard.'

It was Hesseltine. 'Blank, blank and blank.'

'Are you swearing euphemistically, or—'

'Don't make silly jokes, Simon. Twickenham, Stalling Busk, the Dormobile—all blank, not a sausage of evidence and no leads visible—'

'You've found the Dormobile?'

'No. That's a *blank* blank—no sign, vanished into the mists. Never fear—we'll run it to ground somewhere, sometime.'

'Be fast, sir.'

'For what it's worth, we will be.'

'Terry and Nigel—anything on them?'

'CRO reports another blank. First names are not much to go on anyway, and we find no link between a Terry and a Nigel.' The voice of Hesseltine paused. 'One credit: we have Larger—that is, York police have—'

'Great!'

'Don't celebrate too soon. York says he doesn't appear likely to cough. Do you want to confront him yourself, or do we leave it up to York?'

Shard hesitated. 'For the moment, sir, York. I may go up later or I may not. What about his premises?'

A laugh: 'Filthy—but clean in a Hedge sense. No evidence. As a matter of fact, he was caught whilst trying to clean the other filth—by burning. He'd been tipped off by phone from Twickenham, of course, but he was just too late.'

'So York can hold him for a while?'

'They can. There was enough hard porn, when pulped, to keep the Inland Revenue in forms for half a century. Which leads me to this: York's being nicely cagey with him. So far, the grill's along the lines of porn. So far as Larger knows, there's coincidence around and the police haven't necessarily latched on to the other in connexion with him. Query: do we leave it that way for the moment, or do we go in for the big stuff? Want to consult Hedge?'

Shard looked at his wrist-watch. 'Hedge, as I happen to know, is currently attending a dinner at the Netherlands Embassy. I'd sooner not disturb him—too many ears and eyes.'

'Understood, but there's a need for decision, Simon. Can you—?'

'Yes, I can! Hang Hedge. Keep it at porn for now, sir. We may as well tie their minds in such knots as we're left with.' He cut the call, sat for a moment thinking. He was about to reach out for the telephone to put through another call when he heard the sound from outside, very faint: a mere scratch, a scrape ... the scrape, it sounded like, of clothing or a button against woodwork. Grinning tightly, he got to his feet, dead quiet, and moved for the door.

CHAPTER NINE

The door, when jerked open, revealed only flight: a somewhat willowy male form, back view, beating it down the stairs, fast. Could be a client of Elsie's, the lady of the next floor up, but Elsie's clients didn't normally pause outside Shard's door for a button-scratch, nor did they descend quite so precipitously. Anyway, the man had rather more than a head start and Shard knew a chase would be useless. Going to the banisters, he looked down the well of the staircase, keeping in shadow himself: as he had hoped and expected, the running man couldn't resist an upward glance before vanishing out into Seddon's Way and its dustbins.

★   ★   ★

'One of my interrogators, name of Terry, from York and Stalling Busk,' Shard said next morning.

'So you were tailed.' Hedge's voice was disparaging.

'I have to admit the likelihood. Not from the Twickenham house, though. Anybody who got away from there in time to watch me streak, Hedge, would have been worrying not so much about a tail as making sure I didn't get the chance to talk.'

'It doesn't follow.' Hedge jabbed angrily with his umbrella at a discarded and obscene rubber object: this time, the rendezvous had been St James's Park. 'Really, it's quite disgusting. As I was saying . . . there he was—the man! Wasn't he? Where did he pick you up?'

Shard said, 'I don't know. I wish I did. I've been getting around and it could have been anywhere, pure chance.'

'They'll link you with Pearson now, your alias. They'll know *who* Pearson was.'

'No loss. They'd ceased to believe in Pearson anyway! They suspected a cop involvement. And another thing: my philatelic hideout hasn't got my job blazoned over the doorway. Nothing's necessarily blown. It's all grown a shade more confusing for them—that's all!'

Hedge wiped his face. 'That man. I gather he didn't try to get you.'

'No. He listened.'

Hedge gave him a sharp look, sideways. 'What did he hear, Shard?'

'Better ask him. I'm not his ears.'

'You know what I mean.'

Shard sighed. 'Yes, I do. I was on the blower to Assistant Commissioner Hesseltine—'

'That man again!'

'The very same. I doubt if the brilliance of our conversation would have been all that obvious to chummy, though. Except for one

115

thing, which I hate to confess. You're not going to like this, Hedge.'

The small mouth had tightened already. 'Go on, Shard.'

'I spoke your name.'

'Oh God. My *name?*'

'Hedge. Just Hedge.'

Hedge brought a handkerchief and dabbed at sweat on his forehead. 'Jesus Christ. In what connexion?'

'The Netherlands Embassy. I'm sorry, Hedge.'

'Sorry!' Hedge looked as though he were about to cry with one side of his pink face, commit murder with the other: it was a curious sight. 'Oh, my God. Words fail me. They can work out my name now. Two and two ... me, the Netherlands Embassy, last night's reception, the guest list—'

'That's four.'

'What?'

Shard waved a hand, dismissingly. 'Sorry again, Hedge. Look, it's not the end of the world. Nothing important's been blown ... oh. Do I apologise a third time?'

Hedge shook like a high fever. 'I sometimes think this job's beyond you after all, Shard. Yard material—no more.'

'I'd say that to Assistant Commissioner Hesseltine if I were you.'

Hedge hissed, spluttered, scrambled to his

116

feet. 'You—you—*oh, shut up!*' He turned and made off, simmering, legs twinkling along past spring flowers. Shard grinned with a touch of malevolence, hating Hedge for the continuing rift with Beth. Hedge was a bastard ... following his progress in high dudgeon along the path, Shard gave a hoot of delighted laughter: Hedge had the french letter dangling from the ferrule of his umbrella.

★　　★　　★

Cloak-and-dagger was all very well: Shard acknowledged its uses gratefully on occasions—late last night, after the episode of the listening man, he'd indulged in some himself, making a contact down Stepney way. In his job, you couldn't avoid it—but Hedge made it into a fetish, cloaking and daggering his way around town, in and out of the FO and the ministries like a pantomime bad man. He was clever enough in the execution of his tricks but Shard thought it all bloody silly half the time. Like this morning: they both knew the score, both knew they would be meeting anyway inside a couple of hours, but Hedge had been pettish on the phone, notwithstanding the security line, and never mind the urgency of the overall situation either. Protocol had to be kept to; Hedge had to be kept privily informed. Hedge graced the Foreign Office, not one of the common departments: in his own estimation, he ranked as a diplomat, and in point of fact he did have the equivalent rank of Minister of Legation. With men like Hedge obtruding into the system, it was a wonder England survived; but, somehow, she did. Maybe it was simply because of the protocol: the downhill progress would have to proceed by precedent and since there wasn't any the process was precluded from taking place ...

Such mutinous thoughts passed through Shard's mind as he listened, in Hesseltine's office not long after Hedge had seethed away from St. James's Park, to the words of wisdom coming from various pundits. He caught Hesseltine's eye as an elderly Defence Ministry official laid down military law: Hesseltine was looking glazed and, at an appropriate moment, butted in.

'Gentlemen, I must remind you—time is short. We have four days' maximum if the time table is kept to. I have the feeling that some of us don't quite believe the facts. Am I right?'

There was a shuffle of feet, a murmur of voices, some modulated laughter.

'Well, gentlemen?' Hesseltine, eagle-eyed copper, stared round the faces with rising impatient truculence. 'Will you allow me to suggest you cut the cackle and come to something like a decision, or will you give me *carte blanche*?'

Gasps: the gentlemen showed indignation. A voice or two—Defence Ministry, supported by Home Office—murmured that the whole thing was fantasy, that it strained belief, that the precautions currently being taken were more than enough, that the public would become alarmed, that indeed there might be a panic reaction if anything more obvious was done.

Hesseltine, loudly, said, 'That's nonsense. The situation is dangerous in the extreme. Do you not realise?' He thumped the table, glasses of water trembled alongside virgin blotters and sheets of note-taking A4. 'London is faced with the worst threat yet, the threat of a nuclear underground explosion!' Hesseltine simmered, reading the expressions turned towards him: aggrievement, dudgeon, offended dignity. High civil officials didn't take a cry of nonsense from men who had spent a large proportion of their working lives in a blue uniform: Hesseltine was being unseemly. Almost his sole support came from London Transport.

London Transport came in as crisp as one of its own trains crescendoing into Piccadilly: 'Mr Hesseltine's right. We've had the starters, some big, some small. Remember the Old Bailey explosion. Remember the railway stations, remember all those filthy pub bombings. Remember the army coach in Yorkshire, the bomb attacks on military establishments, the Tower, the government offices in Balham. All right—that was all the IRA, and this isn't! Now we're being hit by the other mob. The point is, these things happen, although none of us believed they ever could or would—not in England. England's changing. Only fools won't face the fact!'

'Well, really—'

'Let me tell you something, gentlemen: we in London Transport have always feared something like this. We're wide open to it, and the only wonder is that it hasn't happened long ago. I beg of you to use your imaginations: rivers of blood just won't be in the race! I don't know, I can't suggest, how we combat this. It's not my job to instruct the police—and God knows, they're faced with a big enough task. All we in London Transport can do is to keep up our own security at its top pitch, and co-operate with any extra security the police suggest. But I say again, you must all take the threat very seriously.'

He sat down; Hesseltine nodded his thanks. 'Take due note, gentlemen. Detective Chief Superintendent Shard may help to clear your thoughts, I fancy. Shard?'

Shard, feeling drained by the faces of complacency, got up, leaned his weight on the polished table. 'I've not much to say. We don't know who these people are, where they come from—other than broadly—where they are now. But we're going to dig them out.' He paused. 'This we do know: one Garda officer, one priest and his housekeeper have been murdered. They killed one of their own people—I saw it done. I've been in their hands, was rumbled, got away. I know they exist. I know they will do what they say. I know London is to be blown from underneath. I know all this—there's no argument. Go back to your ministries, tell your chiefs to persuade Government to act. There's no further point in secrecy. I've come round to this view: until we've arrested these people, the whole tube system must be shut down, guarded and patrolled along its whole length by police and troops.'

He caught the eye of Hedge: Hedge, who had remained silent and anonymous, was not pleased. His God was secrecy.

★   ★   ★

In St James's Park station, down on the platform, Hedge said, *sotto voce*, 'I *still* don't agree. You had no business to say that.'

'They don't have to do as I say, though I hope they will.'

Hedge said, 'A one-day closure, as I suggested in the beginning—fair enough. But no longer. It'd be an impossible business. Bring life to a halt.'

'So will the explosion.'

121

'A once and for all thing!' Hedge snapped.

'You don't mean that, Hedge. Not even you.'

'Well . . .' Hedge didn't go on. He gave a sniff of disapproval, glaring round at mixed humanity. 'Another point: unlike you, I don't see that we can blow all secrecy.'

'Not *all* secrecy,' Shard said, heavily patient. 'But we can't avoid the admission that we do *know* about the threat. Not any more—and damn it, I admit my own failures! We're in a position now to take overt precautions. In the public interest, we must take them. That's all.'

Hedge glowered, went off at a tangent. 'Waste of time—that meeting. Talk, talk, talk.'

'Oh, I don't know. It cleared the air a little—I did detect a welcome and salutary sense of fear in some of them, not to say a touch of the dirtied trousers—'

'Shard, really—'

'And how about you?' Shard enquired, grinning.

'Me?'

'You're now slap bang on the underground system—true, this is sub-surface and not deep level, but perhaps you get the feeling?'

Hedge sucked in his cheeks, staring with obvious spite. 'So that's why you talked me into coming down here. It's no damn farther to walk all the way—I told you—'

'Yes,' Shard agreed, still grinning. 'But you don't often use the tubes, so I thought—' He

122

broke off, hearing a distant rumble. 'Here's our train.' In silence they waited for it to pull in. It stopped, a non-smoking door right opposite them. Hedge stepped forward, was halted by Shard's hand on his arm. 'Careful, Hedge!'

'Why?'

'Look!' Shard pointed, face grave now though the eyes were a give-away. 'A Middle Eastern gentleman, Hedge—carrying a parcel.'

Even Shard hadn't expected the instant reaction: Hedge beat it rapidly, and somewhat pointlessly really, for the next carriage along the platform. When he plumped down into a seat, he was quite breathless. He mopped his face and wouldn't speak to Shard. Shard, looking down at the neatly rolled umbrella, saw that the french letter had gone. He wondered if it had been left in Scotland Yard.

★ ★ ★

There was indeed still that point Shard had made to Hedge right at the start, after Casey's body had been found: closure of the system was in a sense pointless, since the Nazarrazeen mob could lie low for a while and then, when the nine-day-wonder was over, come out and start again. Yet, now, it was something that couldn't be avoided, in Shard's view. This, however, a view not shared by the summit. Shard, when Hedge disembarked at

Westminster, went on alone, changing at Charing Cross for Leicester Square, and soon after he reached his office Hedge was on the line.

'Vetoed,' he said. 'He won't have it.'

'He?'

'The Prime Minister. He's been approached—'

'*Already?*'

Hedge sounded reproving. 'There's a certain urgency, is there not? We're not always slow—'

'For God's sake, why the veto? Doesn't he care?'

'I'm quite sure he does, but we must see his point, my dear chap.' Hedge was being patient, though with difficulty. 'He said—so I'm told—we mustn't be seen to be defeated otherwise the country could become ungovernable. I agree, Shard—and so do you really. Look at the hijacks: worse and worse, and will become more so until someone stands up to the demands. He—'

'So London's to be the standing ground, the test case?'

'Well, you could say that, I suppose.'

'I do say it. Christ, Hedge! Couldn't a stance have been taken over something smaller?'

'Agreed—but it wasn't. Now we're stuck with this.' Hedge paused. 'The Prime Minister spoke of Belfast, apparently. Look how they're taking it, he said—'

'They haven't an underground, Hedge.'

'True. But it's been years and years ... and nothing's packed up because of terrorism. It's a point, you know. We mustn't be panicked.'

Shard bared his teeth into the telephone. 'Hedge, you know very well you'll cross the street bloody fast every time you see an Arab from now on.' Angrily, he banged the handset down on its bracket and simmered at it. Terrorism didn't exactly frighten him: he was a copper and terrorism had become a fact of life and had to be faced as such; but in spite of all he had said it did appal him that dedicated nonentities could almost with impunity hold governments, countries, cities to ransom, have whole communities and organisations dancing to their wicked whims, the forces of authority bowing their polite way out backwards while naked savagery went into its sacrosanct performance of death and destruction. Sometime it *had* to stop: maybe the Prime Minister was right, but this time it was going to be too high a price to pay ... the security line burred and before he answered Shard knew who it was: Hedge again, cold and furious at being hung up on.

'You're damn rude, Shard, and I won't have it.'

'I'm sorry.'

'What are you going to *do*?'

Shard jerked his sleeve back and looked at his

watch. 'I'm going north ... to talk to the only possibility we currently have for answering back—'

'Larger?'

'Right, Hedge. I'll hit him with more than porn, a lot more.'

'Keep me informed, won't you?'

'I'll do that. Just as soon as I know anything—'

'Going up by road?'

'British Rail. My car was shot up—remember?'

'I'll arrange a replacement.'

'No. I'll go by train. You never know—something may show.' He paused. 'Hedge?'

'Yes?'

Shard grinned. 'I'm now going to ring off. I thought I'd better tell you, this time.' Hedge's angry snort just reached him before he cut the call. Using his ordinary open line he called Beth: if he hadn't come back into her life the evening before, she'd have been preparing, right now, to go to his funeral.

'Simon,' he said when the call was answered: it was Mrs Micklam. 'How's Beth, mother-in-law?'

'Oh ... getting over it.'

And no thanks to you, he thought. He said, 'I may not be home tonight. If I am, it'll be late. Will you tell Beth, please?'

'Yes, I'll tell her, Simon.'

'You'll still be there, when I get back?'

'If Beth wants me,' she said. There had been a slight and meaningful emphasis on the 'Beth', and he rang off before he became indiscreet—maybe it was the Foreign Office atmosphere, permeating his soul so insidiously ... he would have liked to have said quite a lot, quite a lot. Then, getting up from the untidy desk and going towards his safe, he gave a short, hard laugh. He was a Detective Chief Superintendent, not all that far from the top and young for his rank. If he should become a Deputy Commander CID within the next couple of years, he would be the youngest ever to hold that gilded rank. Yet he had a Mrs Micklam round his neck: the thought, in a sense, intrigued him. To the young PCs on the beat, to the fresh-faced DCs of CID, Detective Chief Superintendents had it made, they had the lot. Overpaid and underworked, shouting the odds down the chain of command, house bought and mortgage repaid, wife waiting with slippers out, you couldn't go wrong. Couldn't you? Shard laughed again: so many unknown crosses from which mere rank couldn't protect you! Envy was a stupid emotion.

★   ★   ★

By tube to King's Cross, openly, no red

herrings: Shard wanted the other side to show, but he got no sign. That could be because he was too open: the fact that he would be expected, sooner or later, to go north for a chat with Larger could operate two ways at once. Shard sat cross-legged in the swaying tube train, reading the adverts, watching his shadowy reflection in the windows backed by the dirty wall of the tunnel, keeping a discreet eye on his current companionship. At the stations people came and went, white, black, yellow, medium. He couldn't lay a mental finger on any, but he knew that danger was with him all the way now. He pressed his left upper arm to his side, liking the feel of the gun in his shoulder-holster: warm, comforting! He listened to the hollow-sounding roar, the train's restless racket, his thoughts sliding on to the greater roar that was to come—*was to come*. No ifs and buts. Shard knew that the security net was tight, couldn't be tighter given that the network was, by Prime Ministerial command, to remain open. But no security was 100 percent; it couldn't be. This world didn't admit perfection. Always the way through—that had been proved time and again by terrorists in many places. When men and women didn't shrink from risking their own lives in a cause, you couldn't, in the last resort, hold them back. They became natural winners...

Shard, very suddenly, caught his breath: his

eye, taken and held by an advert along the coach, a colourful one of the Thames and a river bus going merrily down to Greenwich Pier, had given thought a jolt, sickeningly. *The river.* Good Christ, why hadn't it clicked before now? The maps that London Transport security man had produced—Partington. Three—no, four, wasn't it—four sections of track ... London Bridge to Monument on the Northern Line, Rotherhithe to Wapping on the Metropolitan, and, on the Bakerloo and Northern Lines, twin sections: Waterloo to Charing Cross. *All in tunnels beneath the river.*

Shard felt the sudden sweat break. Deep—yes, those track-bearing river-tunnels would be deep down, of course they would! *But a nuclear explosion?* Shard, horrified now, stared sightlessly back at his darkened image in the train's window as the coach rattled on, next stop King's Cross. Claustrophobic now, it could all happen at any moment, literally. A nuclear blow-out, its lateral movement tamped perhaps, held in—tamping had been specifically mentioned as being part of the job—so that the force went up and outwards, fracturing the tunnel wall, splitting the great weight of London clay, the river bed above. If that fracture should reach the river bottom to be widened by the huge pressure of the water... Shard knew in that moment what it meant to have the mind boggle. Imagination rioted: the huge inroad, the build-up, the solid water rushing unimpeded to infiltrate along the section, then the next section, rising over the platforms of the stations as it spread, rising until it met its own far-overhead level ... the escalators submerging, rattling up from the rising floodwaters, rattling down ... the whole network, the jointures of the different underground systems taking the water to fling it along their own tunnels ... the panic, and the wholesale deaths as men and women and children fought to beat the tumultuous rise. It would be total disaster, the worst ever to hit London since the Great Plague and the Great Fire. This would go down in the history books as the Great Flood.

Shard wiped away the sweat, disembarked like an automaton at King's Cross.

Could it happen? Did it lie only in the mind?

He took a risk—not a large one. From a telephone kiosk he rang London Transport and got Partington. He said, 'Shard. Now listen and interpret. The Thames.'

'The Thames?'

'You know about it,' Shard said, on edge and showing it. 'It's a river.'

'Yes, but—'

'Things below it. Mr Partington, for God's sake get with it! We've talked—you know what about. Could a certain thing happen, or couldn't it?'

A gasp indicated dawning awareness. 'You don't mean—'

'Yes, I do,' Shard said. 'Possible—or not?'

'Good grief, I need warning of this one! Off the cuff I'd say not. It all depends ... on *size*.'

'If it's big—*bloody* big?'

'It'd have to be more than big, I fancy. Colossal. I doubt if it's a starter, Mr Shard. On the other hand ...'

'On the other hand, what?'

'Not impossible. No—not entirely impossible.'

'I check with that, in my non-expert view. I'm going to ask you to do something for me, Mr Partington: go and see Assistant Commissioner Hesseltine—don't ring, go. Tell him what we've talked about.' He rang off, shouldered his way out of the kiosk. The roof of King's Cross station was dirty as ever, but where the glass was not, a bright sun shone, and there was blue sky. Buying a first-class return for York, Shard had a cold feeling, a feeling that the Bible story was about to be reversed upon a godless world: first the sunshine, then the flood.

CHAPTER TEN

Inter-City was fast: Shard, keeping himself to himself in his first-class seat behind a *Daily Telegraph*, found it nevertheless tedious: so much to do, and he could only sit and wait. But in excellent time he was in the nick at York, hearing what he had expected to hear.

'Not the tiniest tickle of a cough, Mr Shard,' the DI reported.

'Porn?'

'That, yes. No alternative, had he?' Gleeson gave a short laugh.

'So he's under no illusions—he knows he'll be going down on the porn charge, I take it?'

The DI said, 'He knows! Is that in accordance with—'

'With my wishes—yes. It's not a bad handle, as handles go, and we haven't many yet.' Shard stood up. 'May I talk to him?'

'Well, that's why you've come, isn't it? You may, but...'

'But what, Inspector?'

'What, exactly, are you going to do, Mr Shard?'

Briefly, Shard grinned. 'No coughing—now, that condition needs a starter! I'm going to give the bastard a sore throat. Oh, it's your patch, Inspector, and I've no quarrel with that. But I have the authority to say this: just while I'm in that charge room with Mr Larger, it's going to be a little piece of York that's forever London—or anyway, Whitehall.'

★   ★   ★

'Well now, Mr Larger.'

'Well now what?' Brave words, truculently said, but the face was a give-away: Larger was rattled.

Shard signed to the uniformed constable standing back against the door, hands behind his rump. The PC left, clicking the door to. Shard, sitting at a plain table facing the porn merchant, smiled. 'Now I'll tell you well now what! We've met, we both know that—'

'Why bother to say it, then?'

Shard smiled on. 'Just a lead-in. You've been contacted by some villains in Twickenham, of course, but I take it you still don't know who I am. Do you?' He shot the question, bullet-like, the smile snapping off blank. He repeated it: 'Do you, Mr Larger?'

Larger licked his lips. 'A bloody jack.'

'Good guess. Let me fill you in. A bloody jack by the name of Shard, Detective Chief Superintendent. In the Metro, Mr Larger, they still speak of me as Iron Shard.'

'Do they?' Sharp eyes glittered from the pasty face, a face that shone just a little with fresh sweat.

'Oh, they do indeed,' Shard said ruminatively, rocking back on the rear legs of his chair. He came down fast, hands flat on the table. 'And with reason. There's a reason for everything, isn't there, Mr Larger?'

'If you say so.'

'I say so. There's even a reason for you. A reason for you to be here. Right?'

'Course. Why waste time? They nicked me and that's it.'

'For porn.'

'Yes.'

'Then let's talk about porn, Mr Larger.'

Larger shrugged. 'If you want.' He gave a snigger, a salacious noise. 'If you want a thrill, look at the stock.'

'It doesn't really thrill me.'

'No? There's all sorts, all tastes catered for, heteros, homos, lesbians, gang bangs—'

'Shut up,' Shard said. 'You make a man vomit.'

'I thought the fuzz enjoyed the pickings. All spread out on the front office counter ... WPCs and all—'

'Think again, then. It's a laugh, that's all—a bitter one, sometimes, thinking of all the dirty money involved. All the same, I want to talk about porn, so we'll talk about it, all right?'

Larger shrugged his disinterest, but the eyes had narrowed and the pasty cheeks had a suspicion of a wobble. 'We said, we'd met. You haven't come to talk about porn. Not really.'

'No?' Shard rose to his feet, stood for a moment looking down at Larger, running his eyes slowly over the whole man, face, thick square body, the bison's shoulders, back again to the shiny baldness of the head. After this, he took a turn around the charge room, round the table, round behind Larger, beneath the metal-barred window, past the paintwork of police green. He stopped behind Larger, bent over the strong shoulders. 'I have, you know!'

'No need to shout,' Larger said.

'All right, I won't. Porn—it's a nasty business, shouldn't be shouted aloud, I quite agree. Very nasty, and you're in deep. It isn't the first charge ... I checked, so don't waste breath. The police have known you for years, Larger, and just lately they've been keeping you on ice—for which I'm truly thankful. This time, you're going inside so fast—'

'On a porn charge?'

'On a porn charge—you know the law as well as I do—'

'You'll need the Attorney-General's—'

'Don't worry about him, I don't. There are other charges too: living off immoral earnings, procuring, just to name two. You're dirty, Larger. Just think about prison: think hard, and come to some conclusions, right?'

'Like what?'

'Like: certain people, certain other people unconnected with porn, aren't going to be happy with you. Even our high security prisons can't be sure of protecting nice, prime targets like you. You—'

'We're getting there, aren't we? You know some of it. All right, I won't deny what I can't deny. But I'm not saying anything more and you won't make me by your sort of tactics.' Larger waved a hand, loftily. 'These people you spoke of. They won't try to get me—why should they? Not if I don't cough! Don't come to me for help, Mr Shard, because I'm not grass green.'

'I didn't think you were,' Shard said. 'And I wasn't talking about your explosive friends, who I presume have made promises, however worthless, to keep you in comfort when you come out, just so long as you haven't given them away—'

'Right.'

Shard laughed, and sat down again facing Larger. 'If you believe that,' he said, 'you're greener than any grass I've ever seen. When you come out, they aren't going to be around any more!'

'Their backers are, Mr Shard.'

'And they're—who?'

Larger's mouth clamped down hard, lips together in a thin and meaningful line. Shard said carelessly, 'Never mind, we can make a good guess. Perhaps you'd like to know who the people are you should start worrying about.'

'Try me.'

Shard said, 'Your fellow cons. You're going down for a long time—that's for certain sure, and even you don't doubt it. Even clever bent lawyers won't get you out of that, and for my part I don't doubt you have some tame ones lined up ready.' He paused, staring into Larger's half-shut eyes. 'Inside, you're going to suffer. I'm going to see to it that you live through bloody hell, and that no complaint you ever make is listened to by the screws or the Governor. Don't get me wrong: I don't bluff. These things I can do—'

'You're a bastard,' Larger said flatly.

'But clearly a believable bastard. Yes, I'm a bastard when I have to be, when it's in a good cause. You know how big this thing is, don't you?'

Larger didn't answer that.

'A lot of people will die if it's allowed to happen.' Shard paused, then added, 'By drowning, some of them. Right, Larger?'

There was no reaction, no flicker.

'Wise men see the red light in time, Larger. Your time is running out. I know your involvement—and you know I know. You can stop this happening—or help to stop it—by talking. Cast your so-called friends from your mind, Larger. When it suits them, they'll cast you quick enough. In the meantime, you'll be in custody waiting trial on the porn charge, I shall see to that. Then you'll go down—and the cons you meet inside will know the truth. I'll see that they know it, Larger. Now, it's a fair bet that some of them are going to have friends or relatives, even wives and children, who'll have been killed by your friends, killed by something in which you'll have been involved, something you could have stopped and didn't. London's a big place, Larger. Fourteen million possibilities. There's a thing called the law of averages—remember?'

Still no reaction, beyond a look that had grown slightly more wary. Shard got to his feet, stood looking down at the seated man. 'Cons ... men helpless in high security prisons. A mother or father—a wife, a child as I said—is killed by senseless terrorism while they're held inside prison walls. Then you turn up among them. You're the man, the physical embodiment of what happened—never mind that you didn't set the charges! And even screws are human. I'd think about it, Larger.'

He turned away, opened the door, beckoned the constable. 'Lock the swine up,' he said. 'Two men, and handcuffs—I'll be having another word with your DI.' He glanced back at Larger. 'Don't forget your wife. All my remarks apply equally to her.'

At last, a reaction: 'Ethel's not in this, they

didn't bring her in even.'

'Not the porn—they didn't bother. I'll be seeing her, Larger.'

Larger's face was white. 'You know something? You won't ... not at home.'

Shard felt rocked: the tick-over had been fast but late. Of course! He said, 'You mean—'

'You know what I mean, Mr Shard. Can't you see, that's why I can't talk—or one of the reasons?' He lifted his arms, let them drop again. 'What would happen to Ethel, Mr Shard?'

★ ★ ★

'We slipped,' Shard said savagely, feeling personal about it. 'Not your fault, Inspector—I should have been in touch right away. In a sense, this is an impasse so far as Larger's concerned.'

'If we can get to her—'

'Which we can't, until we get the whole bunch. That's the point!' Shard smashed a fist into his palm. 'We've lost our lead to them or what might have been a lead! After it's over ... it'll be too bloody late, won't it? Oh, I put it to Larger that his wife's best hope was to be found before anything could happen, but he—'

'Doesn't have much faith in the police?' The Inspector laughed, hollowly. 'What villain has? They all know their own kind, stands to reason.

So what's next, Mr Shard?'

Shard didn't answer directly. He turned away, stared out of a window, seeing nothing that registered, occupied with milling thoughts and anxieties, seeing the red horror pressing out and up below London, the Thames itself erupting in a great atomic blast, and then the rushing thunderous waters, trapping, cutting off, smashing bodies in its torrent ... he saw the faces of fear, faces swept away, torn from the platforms to be hurled willy-nilly into the bursting tunnels. Sweat broke out. The DI cut into his thoughts.

'Suppose we let Larger go, sir?'

Shard turned. 'A tail? Too risky, too obvious all round. Too many snags.'

'I think, if we leaked it that he'd been released, these people would show.'

'I say again, too risky. While we have him, there's always a chance he'll cough. For my money, that's a better risk. I'd say a show on their part is doubtful now—too obviously expected.'

'We're not dealing with professionals, Mr Shard. They won't have normal villain reactions. Amateurs tend to rush in—we all know that. I believe they'd show, and we'd have a chance of copping the whole bang shoot.'

'Well, we'll keep it in mind,' Shard said. 'In the meantime, keep up the pressure I began, and don't kid-glove the bastard.'

The DI nodded. 'Will do. And you, sir?'

'Back to London like a yo-yo. My job's supposed to be security pure and simple and I reckon we may not have much longer. I'll leave you to the trail up here while I concentrate on prevention in the south. Keep in touch, Inspector.'

★   ★   ★

Telephones, telephones, telephones: this time, within two seconds of reaching home, and it was the inevitable Hedge.

'Shard, really! I've been ringing—'

'I've been in a train. This, you know very well.'

'All right, all right. You're wanted, and you're wanted now. I—'

'Where and why, Hedge?'

'My place. Please don't delay.' There was a pause. 'The *back* door.' Hedge rang off, not having answered the question why, but Shard was willing to admit that could have been a silly question. He glowered at the phone: back door, indeed! Hedge cloak-and-daggering, or the slight of the tradesmen's entrance? He went over to his wife, bent and kissed her. 'Sorry, darling—'

'But you have to go out again.'

'Yes.'

'How long this time?'

141

He said, 'I can't say.' He stood up, looked down at the top of her head, at the source of the long fair hair, long like that of Nadia Nazarrazeen ... something welled up in Shard as he stood there looking at his wife: he wanted, and wanted desperately, to tell her the facts of a desperate situation. Ealing ... oh, it wasn't central London, not by a long chalk, but Beth didn't confine herself to Ealing or parts adjacent. She liked the West End shops and a cup of tea in one of the big stores. When the crunch came, London's very foundations could be shaken—and Beth travelled around by tube mostly.

She watched his face, frowning a little. 'What's the matter, Simon?'

'Why d'you ask that?'

'You look ... sort of funny.'

He grinned. 'Do I? I don't feel it. For a dead man—' He broke off: that was *not* funny. 'Sorry, darling. Sorry if I look funny, too. But a policeman's lot...' He avoided her eyes, looked away across the room, comfortably furnished, with a lived-in look and at the moment domestic: Mrs Micklam was sewing, surrounded by reels of cotton spilling from a work bag on the sofa, eyes down, pretending to the young people that she wasn't there. Shard considered her balefully. She was not the most discreet of women. Even a vague warning, a suggestion that for a while the West End might with profit be avoided, wasn't on: when Detective Chief Superintendents, like the Captains of H.M. ships in wartime, gave vague warnings, intrigued minds grew too busy. Then it came to him, and remembering the waiting Hedge, he lost no more time.

'You look tired, Beth. You've had too much worry the last few days—my fault, was that. Why not have a week or so away? Get out of town?' He added the rest with a touch of reluctance he couldn't quench: 'Stay with your mother. How about that, Beth?'

Mrs Micklam's sewing finger slowed. Beth glanced across at her, then at Shard. There was pleasure in her eyes: a few days on the south coast would be nice. She said, 'That's good of you, Simon. I'll talk it over with Mummy.'

He left her to do that, feeling that very probably she wouldn't: she was a good wife, was Beth, and knew that busy top coppers hadn't the time or the inclination to do for themselves. Maybe he would have to be a little more insistent when he got back: to have her in the clear would greatly relieve his mind and he would find it convenient enough to snatch pub meals as and when he could. Proceeding Hedgeward by underground, he felt the loss of his car: Hedge's kind offer of replacement might now be accepted. He left the underground at Victoria and walked fast to Eaton Square, which had the honour of

143

containing Hedge's flat: a flat it was, though Hedge always referred to it as 'my house' or 'my place' because in fact his family had once owned and inhabited it as a complete house, back in the spacious days, the days when the family had had almost as many indoor servants as their latter-day scion had policemen. Obeying orders, Shard slunk round the back, up a service alley and across the garden to the back door: more like a cat burglar than an honest tradesman really, for the tradesmen's entrance was actually in the front area. He was admitted by Hedge's manservant, Morton.

'Good evening, sir.' His face was familiar to Morton, infrequent though house visits were. 'The master is in the study—'

'Right, Morton, I'll find my own way, thanks.' Shard went through the nether regions, through a green baize door, into the hall, into Hedge's study, a comfortable room lined with books in massive mahogany bookcases. Hedge was standing with his back to the fireplace, below a portrait of an earlier and splendidly uniformed Hedge. Alongside him was Hesseltine and sitting in a worn leather armchair was Partington of London Transport.

'Ah, Shard.'

'Good evening, Hedge.' Shard nodded at the other two.

'Any luck in York?' Hedge asked.

'Not yet. I have hopes.'

'Enough to bank on?'

'I wouldn't say quite that.'

Hesseltine glanced at Hedge, who was fingering pink facial flesh and looking anxious. Hesseltine said, 'As a matter of fact, Simon, I've been in touch with York since you left them. Larger's been taken ill.'

'Oh, God! Bad?'

Hesseltine nodded. 'Heart, they tell me. A sudden collapse. He's been moved to the intensive care unit in the local hospital. There's a DC on watch, but of course he's not allowed any contact. It's a sod ... but there it is. If we had a bank, it's closed its doors, for the time being anyway. In the meantime, we have other matters to think about.'

'What matters in particular?'

Hesseltine pointed a cigar at Partington. 'Your idea of a fractured under-river tunnel, Simon.'

'Well, sir?'

'We rather think it could be on. That is—we don't rule it out. Mr Partington?'

Partington spoke to Shard, his chin resting on the tips of his fingers, held parsonwise. 'After you rang, I did some homework. Those four sections you mentioned—they're deep, all but one. That one's the Rotherhithe to Wapping on the Metropolitan, the East London as we call it. It's near enough to the surface to have fairly constant seepage even without an explosion, Mr Shard, but—'

'But it wouldn't be very significant?'

'Significant?'

Shard elaborated: 'Not as busy a line as the others, not so central—not so casualty-prone on the wider scale. Not enough *potential*—it's sub-surface, isn't it, not deep level?'

'Yes, that's true, but the others—they're really deep, Mr Shard—'

'How deep?'

'It varies. Between 25 and 45 feet below the river bed. The bed's solid. It's a lot of earth to blow.'

'But you don't, I gather, rule it out.' Shard looked towards Hedge. 'I made a certain report to you earlier, Hedge, about the explosion potential. Has Mr Partington . . . ?'

Hedge nodded. 'Yes, he knows.'

Shard said, 'In that case . . . Mr Partington, when I telephoned you, you said it all depended on size. Well?'

The London Transport man was grey-faced with anxiety, seemed almost unable to utter the words of truth. 'If it's to be nuclear, Mr Shard, I believe it can be done. In fact I'd say . . . certainly it can be done. Again size must come into it, and the availability—'

Shard broke in: his earlier visit to the US Embassy had been very fruitful. 'I've been looking up the records and studying figures. I've concentrated on America, land of the Fast

Breeder Reactor. The United States Atomic Energy Commission has been getting in a panic over disappearances during the last year or so—portable containers have been stolen from plants holding stocks of fissionable material such as refined plutonium. There's plenty of that around, produced by neutron bombardments of Uranium 238 in the Fast Breeders. As I dare say you know, the Fast Breeder produces more plutonium than it burns uranium, which is why it's called the Fast Breeder. And I think we all know, too, that the difficulty in producing a nuclear explosion lies in actually making the fissionable material. Given that, any schoolboy with an adequate knowledge of physics and chemistry can make the bomb itself—'

'But—'

'One moment, Mr Partington. After the last Arab–Israeli dust-up, the AEC got its General Accounting Office to check security—just in case, and this is I believe relevant, some of its stocks could have reached the Middle East—'

'And had they?'

Shard said, 'We don't know. But we do know the GAO found that overall security, though good on the surface, was as full of flaws as a dog of fleas—I won't go into detail but the GAO investigators took just half a minute to cut their way into the steel-walled building where the containers were stored. No one knows where the leak about *that* occurred, but the reports I've read indicate that before security could be tightened, a frightening quantity of their fissionable materials was in fact stolen. And I say again, it doesn't take much know-how to make up something with the blast power of what the Americans used to flatten Hiroshima: you even have a choice, as a matter of fact—the refined plutonium, or enriched uranium, no more than would go easily into a conventional suit-case ... not a remarkable piece of equipment on the London underground!'

'But the handling dangers—the radiation, the gamma rays—'

'I understand,' Shard interrupted, 'that three casing layers take care of that virtually 100 percent: lead, biological concrete, more lead. The protection is in fact 99.9 percent.'

Hedge massaged his chin. 'All this ... you're speaking basically of America,' he said in a disparaging tone.

'I am, Hedge. There's plenty of traffic between America and the Middle East, and between America and London. It's not in isolation. Terrorism's spreading, terrorists are proliferating—'

'We're concerned with one group only, Shard.'

'Check. But they're part of the whole. They're amateurs, but we know there's a degree of co-ordination, a kind of clearing-house if you

148

like. There could be central stock-holders—probably somewhere in the Middle East.'

'But these people in particular—there's no American connexion?'

'Not that we know of,' Shard said. 'Nazarrazeen's not known there—not under that name, and nothing's come in from the description. But we still don't know the names of the others.'

There was a silence, broken by Assistant Commissioner Hesseltine. 'So what do we do? Ideas, Hedge?'

Hedge lifted his arms helplessly, let them drop again. Shard came in: 'We regard the under-river sections as the most likely—'

'But not exclusively so.' This was Hedge.

'I didn't say that, Hedge. Full security, all over. But with a very special awareness about the river.' Shard turned to Partington. 'I'll need a very full briefing,' he said. 'Let's start with antidotes, shall we? Do you in fact have any anti-flood system? Has this kind of thing ever been considered?'

Partington shook his head. 'We've never thought in terms of a blow-out from inside, no. But there was the war, of course—'

'The bombing?'

'Yes. The powers that were, had certain anxieties about the possible effects of ordinary bombing—'

'Germane to this?'

Partington nodded. 'Yes. They were worried about direct flooding from the river if the tunnels should be breached. You'll remember people used the underground stations as shelters during the blitz.'

'Yes. So?'

'Action was taken to contain any flooding—or try to. In the event it never happened—'

'What action?'

'Watertight doors,' Partington said. 'They still exist. The tunnels can be closed off at either end. It's cumbersome, but it's said to work.'

'Quickly? How quickly, from the first alarm?'

'Inside thirty seconds.'

'Fast,' Shard said. 'But probably not fast enough. Don't forget the vital point: this is going to come from inside, not out. It's a big difference. How vulnerable is the closing mechanism, Mr Partington?'

Partington said heavily, 'It very likely wouldn't stand up to what we've been talking about, but I thought it worth mentioning.'

Absently, Shard nodded: the watertight doors didn't sound too useful. Any terrorist worth his salt would have taken the trouble to case what looked like being the biggest joint of all time. Partington filled in the gaps: all details were confined to the Top Secret files, but the value of that was highly doubtful: too many people worked in the system, and there was no longer the moral wartime clamp on careless talk that might cost lives: and less reputable citizens could talk for gain. If the river tunnels were to be the target, the watertight doors would have ways around them, and not only for the rushing floodwater: if they were thought to be not susceptible to the main explosion, they could presumably have their own personal and smaller charges set in place. There had been—what?— four men, according to Tom Casey, to carry the explosives. And of course there could be more than one main attack area, too. Shard went into the operational set-up of London Transport: time tables, frequencies in and out of the rush hours. It was a complex, dove-tailing business and would call for detailed study as soon as possible, but for now Partington's general statement of timing sufficed: a train every two-and-a-half to three minutes during rush hours, every four to five minutes in the slack times. The tunnels in the river bed sections were of twelve-foot-six diameter; and the construction was of cast-iron segments bolted into a ring built up within a shield, the space between the cast iron and London's clay layer being filled by the in-pumping of a cement-and-sand grout. There was plenty of room for an explosion to spread and dissipate: the result could still be unacceptably high casualties, but the lateral spread might well save the walls of the chosen tunnel or tunnels...

'All this,' Hedge said reasonably enough, 'pre-supposes that they *do* mean to breach the river-tunnel. And that, we don't know!'

'Agreed,' Shard said wearily: his head ached badly, like a ticking bomb itself. Hedge had produced whisky, but too meanly for decent effects: they were all flying on one wing. 'As I said, I'm working just on the assumption—until we get something harder, anyway.'

'But they'd *know* about this—this lateral dissipation,' Hedge insisted, moving restlessly about by the fireplace. 'They'd know it and go for something simpler—for plain casualties along a crowded platform, *anywhere else* in the system—not something with such difficulties—'

'I don't agree. They did talk of tamping, Hedge, packing the explosion tightly, if you remember my report—very specific, they were.'

'They can't *tamp* a twelve-foot tunnel!' Hedge snapped.

'Not easily, I agree. I'm keeping an open mind, Hedge.'

'I'm glad to hear it.' Hedge, reluctantly, moved towards the whisky decanter. 'What do you propose to do, my dear fellow?'

Shard said, 'I'd like to ... thanks, Hedge.'

Hedge had poured one finger. 'Like to what?'

'Do a survey of my own, Hedge.'

'Of the underground itself, d'you mean?' Hedge stood with the decanter poised towards Hesseltine. 'I suggest, the sooner the better.'

152

'Right away, if Mr Partington will act as guide,' Shard said. 'Night time's the only chance we'll get—unless the Prime Minister can be persuaded to shut down the system.'

Hedge made an angry ejaculation; as he did so the study door opened and his wife came in wearing a quilted dressing-gown. Politely, the men got to their feet: Shard, who had met Mrs Hedge before, wondered wickedly if even she called Hedge Hedge. Hedge looked irritated at the sight of her. In a tight voice he said, 'Yes, dear?'

'I'm sorry to interrupt,' she began. She was fairly sexless, with straggly grey bedtime hair and a heavy face, a bovine manner: but she was well-connected, which was maybe why Hedge had married her—there were earls in the background, somewhere, and stately homes to provide rest for work-weary Hedges when occasion demanded. 'He needs his sleep,' she said, smiling an apology at the others, who responded with vaguely sympathetic murmurs.

Hedge put down the decanter. 'I won't be long, dear. It's not that late anyway. If I were you, I'd go to bed,' he added crossly, looking embarrassed. Mrs Hedge smiled around the study again and drifted off, but her visitation had had its effect, had come between Hedge and the consideration of the national interest: he didn't say so, but he wanted them all to go. Shard glanced at Partington, who nodded: the

153

guide was willing. Hedge, however, had one more thing to say.

'Shard, there's the question of Larger. If he would talk, all the corners could be cut.'

'How I agree!' Shard said, 'But for the time being, we've lost him, haven't we?'

Hedge pursed his lips, looked down at the floor. 'I wouldn't say so entirely, no.'

'You want me to put the boot in, Hedge? Into a sick-room?'

'Well...'

'Doctors are doctors, they have the final say. In any case, I don't like it.'

'There's more than Larger's life at stake, Shard. Just think about it.' After that, the dismissal was clear and obvious: they left singly to Hedge's instructions, Hesseltine by the front door. Shard, walking down to Sloane Street, hailed a passing taxi. He was dropped by the Ritz Hotel; when the taxi drove off he walked on to Piccadilly Circus tube station. He waited: there were still plenty of people around, he knew he wouldn't stand out too much. Waiting, he thought about Larger: Hedge was being a right bastard again, but maybe a *right* bastard—in another sense. You couldn't be squeamish when a whole metropolitan population was potentially at stake, and Larger was hardly worth much consideration. And the imminence of death could prove a loosener of tongues—*could*. When the sword was poised, men changed—or so it was said. They might decide it was a pleasant thing after all, to sit on the right hand of God the Father Almighty. Not that Larger, porn merchant plus, was likely to have got religion in any really big way...

Shard, coming back to Piccadilly, felt an eye upon him: a sharply curious eye beneath a blue helmet, slowly moving in. He cursed, wished Partington would hurry with his master keys and his authorisations, the wherewithal to enter London's night-shut underground—which, right here, was much too suggestive of a public lavatory.

The blue helmet stopped; hands behind back, portly stomach rising and falling upon lifting heels, the intrusive copper probed. 'May I ask your business, sir?'

Shard said, 'No, you may not. But I'm not a pouf and I'm not importuning.' Just at the wrong moment, Partington came along Piccadilly like approaching an assignation, and Shard fumed: just in case of accidents, Hedge's people didn't normally carry official identification. This could take time.

*   *   *

The call from Hesseltine brought Hedge out of bed at seven thirty, eyes crusted with sleep and Mrs Hedge a motionless mountain left isolated in linen. 'Hedge. What is it?'

155

'Hesseltine. Two new items. Ready?'

'Oh, get on with it!'

'Your man almost got arrested for importuning for immoral purposes—'

'Great God!'

'—but that was sorted out. The other's not so easy: Larger.'

'Well?'

'A team of white coats ... very medical, very Sir Lancelot Spratt.' A pause: Hesseltine liked drama. 'Larger's dead, stone cold. So is a sister. And a registrar. And another DC. The weapon used was a scalpel, right to the heart in each case. And another patient dead from shock. No clues of any sort, one scalpel left behind but clean of prints—rubber gloves, of course. There's something else, something you won't like.'

'Tell me.' Hedge's voice was showing the strain.

'The Press has got hold of it, Hedge.'

'Oh, no!' Panic sounded: the Press was Hedge's mortal enemy, the signal set for failure. 'I'll put the stopper on—I'll get—'

'Too late. It happened in good time for the Late News, Stop Press, whatever your newspaper likes to call it. Go down to breakfast and have a look.'

'I will. Look, what are these people *after*? Haven't you any ideas?'

There was a laugh. 'Your job, is that. What

156

springs to mind is some sort of national blackmail, and that's almost too obvious to state.'

The line was cut. Hedge stood trembling with indecision.

CHAPTER ELEVEN

Walking the silent underground had been the eeriest of night experiences: an empty station, closed booking hall with shuttered windows, the escalators motionless, the girls in scanty underwear staring from unappreciated adverts, showing their almost all to the desert air. Voices, kept lowered as though in church, tended to echo even so. Shard and Partington, after an infuriating visit to West End central nick, walked down the escalator one behind the other, waited on the dim platform for the arrival of the maintenance gang's train that would take them to Charing Cross. The train's racket was heard long before its arrival, a weirdly rising sound in the stillness. It cascaded in, stopped to take the two passengers aboard: workmen of London Transport stared without much interest, carrying their mealtins and thermos flasks of tea, bags of tools on oily seats beside them, air thick with smoke. Discreetly Shard studied the faces: like the rest of workaday London, all colours from Tide white to deepest black, but no one who looked like the Middle East. That didn't have to mean much: Shard tried not to think that what was going to happen, could happen tonight. They rattled on, swaying, not talking now. The train decanted them at Charing Cross, along with some of the maintenance men, then roared away into the tunnel. The gangs dispersed about their business and Shard followed Partington towards a locked telephone box. The security man opened it up and made a brief call.

Ringing off and leaving the box unlocked, he said, 'They'll call back when the current's off.'

'No more workmen's trains?'

Partington shook his head. 'Not on this section.'

They waited: a long wait—Partington said, until the train they'd come in had cleared the length of track that would be affected by the power cut-off. When the confirming call came, the jangle shattered the silence horribly. Partington answered, acknowledged, re-locked the box.

'All safe, Mr Shard.'

Down onto the line, along the track: Shard remembered the traditional advice to drunks: don't pee on the live rail. Walking close, trousers touching from time to time, he shivered. If and when the blow-up came, if it was what he feared, killing doses of power were

158

going to be water-borne like lightning along the system before someone cut the supply.

Into the tunnel, into thick, thick darkness sliced by a powerful beam from Partington's workmanlike torch. A stale smell, a smell of metal and grime and damp: they moved on, stumbling over the rails of the four foot eight-and-a-half inch gauge: two conductor rails, in the centre a negative that was nominally at 220 volts below neutral, at the side of the track a positive, nominally at 440 volts above neutral; the negative rail was held on the centre of the jarrahwood sleepers by porcelain insulators, the positive being held in insulators on special wooden blocks sunk into the concrete that on the deep tracks took the place of the ballast used in the open sections and in the sub-surface tunnels of such lines as the District. The running rails, Partington said, were delivered in 60-foot lengths and welded into 300-foot sections at the Fulham depot, where a flash-butt welding machine was used. The live rails were in up to half-mile lengths: traction current was collected by top contact on supply from sub-stations linked by 33kW cables to Lots Road, Greenwich and Neasden, the London Transport power stations. As they went along Partington talked of the system's complexity, of the criss-cross pattern, the varying levels, of the intricacies of the signalling devices and controls—the automation, the two-aspect colour lights and train stops, de-energised track circuits, route control, coded track circuits using pulses of four frequencies to regulate speed, apply emergency brakes and re-start trains.

'How about telephone communication?' Shard asked.

'From driver to controller?'

'Yes. Wires, isn't it?'

Partington said, 'Wires, yes. Emergency use ... the driver reaches out—there's a pair of wires running along the walls—he just nips them together, that causes a short that sounds the alarm at the substation and cuts the juice. Then the driver hitches on his portable telephone, and says what he has to say. If he wants to bypass the substation and speak direct to the controller he can similarly connect up his *permanent* telephone—that's also in the cab—and use the radio frequency carrier waves—'

'Not true radio communication?'

'No. That's not practicable, not inside the iron tubes.' Partington went on to talk of other things, the lurking things with equal rights beneath London's surface, things Shard already had much in mind: sewers, electricity cables, gas mains, fresh water pipes, a whole nerve-centre jumble that sustained the life of the capital. But essentially, that problem had been faced many, many times in the war: plain surface bombs also dug deep into the spider's-web of mains services, the mod cons of sophisticated living. They were important, but they were not people.

'Up there now,' Partington said suddenly, giving his torch an upwards flick.

'What?'

'The river.'

Shard examined the walls in the torchlight. Dry enough, in spite of the overall feeling of pervasive damp. Dry and solid, well down in the river bed: wrong tree? Without a doubt, the feeling of solidarity argued against success for terrorism. Partington expanded on the flood-holding devices, never yet used. Vastly thick doors, iron filled with concrete, electrically operated by remote control, would descend through heavy rubber seals from the roof to slot down firmly into the floor of the track, at either side of the Thames.

He showed Shard where: there was little visible evidence of the descent slots. The seals were flush, grimed to be as one with the tunnel's basic construction.

Shard asked, 'What do you really think?'

'Whatever I think,' was Partington's grim reply, 'it's not only the best we can do, it's *all* we can do—at this stage.'

'It's not enough.' Shard took the torch himself, looked long and close, then shook his head. 'It's too bloody vulnerable! It'll jam up in the first split-second after the explosion.'

'You sound as if we're beaten before it starts.'

Shard gave a ghost of a laugh. 'In a sense, one always is! Have you ever heard of an unsuccessful attempt by terrorists?'

'As a matter of fact, yes, I have. They haven't always pulled it off—not when aircraft have been involved, anyway.'

Shard grinned without humour. 'I'll tell you something, Mr Partington: when aircraft have been involved, there's been a definite requirement on the part of the hijackers. This time, we're not dealing with hijackers. And a tube tunnel isn't Heathrow, or Kennedy.' He shone the beam down along the track, into the endless gloom. 'We'll get back up top. This place ... it gives me the creeps.'

★   ★   ★

Hedge, for once disdaining the telephone, had come on a stamp-buying mission to Seddon's Way, in person. On arrival he'd slumped into a rickety chair, looking grey rather than pink, a bowler hat still on his head and his umbrella clasped like a Boy Scout's stave, upright from the floor. He had ticked Shard off about the importuning, realistically.

'A bad show, you know.'

'Now look here—'

'Oh, I'm not accusing you of *doing* it! But you

162

should be much more *circumspect*.'

'If I want to make a date?'

Hedge glowered. 'Don't joke, I don't like it. You know very well what I mean. It's your job not to arouse suspicions, isn't it?'

Shard blew out a long breath. 'Yes, Hedge. I'm sorry, Hedge, three bags full. Rebuke accepted. Now—what have you come about?'

Hedge coughed, sneezed loudly, brought out his handkerchief and blew his nose. 'Larger's dead,' he said.

'What?' Shard half rose, holding the arms of his chair.

'I thought that would shake you.' Hedge smirked.

'Oh, get on with it! Dead—his heart?'

'Yes. A scalpel in it. Murdered, my dear fellow. He's not going to talk now, is he?' Hedge explained, his tone heavy with undeserved blame: he always had to have someone to blame, and Shard disliked undeserved blame as much as anyone else. There was nothing he, Shard, could have done to safeguard Larger in an intensive care unit, especially from London. York police were not incapable of managing their own affairs, would not have appreciated nanny on the telephone. Just the same, a blow was a blow; and Shard, pondering on the fresh killings, wondered how he'd come to be so lucky himself—maybe he was being preserved for a good reason, a deal or

163

a safeguard, a handy bargaining counter if, one day, he were taken alive: who could tell? Meanwhile Hedge was talking on. 'Mean to say you've not read the newspapers?'

'No, I haven't. They've got Larger's death, have they?'

'They have, in the Stop Press. God alone knows what the evenings would have said if I hadn't stepped in,' Hedge said fervently. 'The Stop Press merely reported a hospital killing—I've put a security clamp on the details. We don't want a sensation and a lot of questions just now, do we?' He blew his nose once again. 'What about the tube tunnels, Shard? Find anything, did you?'

'They were as bare as a whore's bottom.'

'Shard, *please.*'

'You didn't expect me to *find* anything, did you?'

'Well—no, perhaps not. But did you form any conclusions, any—'

'Only depressing ones.' Shard told Hedge all about his night walk beneath London and its river, about his reservations regarding the effectiveness of the anti-flood precautions. 'Last war,' he said briefly. 'Times have moved on. Back in the war, at the time of the blitz that is, they weren't thinking in terms of nuclear explosions.'

'True.' Hedge gnawed anxiously at his lower lip. 'What do we do about Larger, Shard?'

164

'Bury him, presumably.'

'You know what I mean!'

'Yes, I do.' Shard rubbed at tired, red-rimmed eyes: last night, no sleep at all. 'I don't see any point in my going north again, not unless I get some leads from York police. I think we have to forget Larger, Hedge.'

'We've got to do *something*!'

'I shall be,' Shard said. 'With your approval, of course.'

'Well?'

'We haven't got far, working from the outside in. It's time we worked from the inside out, and that's what I propose doing. To do it, I'll need to denude the department of all officers, Hedge. I'll need them all to work with me.'

'Whatever you say,' Hedge said.

'Thanks! I've already been in touch with Assistant Commissioner Hesseltine, pending your okay. There'll be the fullest co-operation from the Yard and from Partington of London Transport—'

'Doing what, Shard?'

'I'm joining in with what Hesseltine and Partington are already doing: watching *in situ*. I'm going underground, Hedge, till this thing's over. I want to catch them all red-handed.'

★　　★　　★

165

When Hedge had gone, Shard rang Beth. 'You'd be better off to do as I suggested,' he said. 'It's going to continue this way for a while yet.'

'How long, Simon?'

'I can't say. Long enough I shouldn't wonder—'

'I'd sooner stay.'

'I'd sooner you went, Beth. Really.'

She said, with an uneasy laugh. 'You do sound anxious, Simon darling!'

'I am. I worry about you—about not getting back when I say, I mean—'

'I'm quite used to that.'

'Sure—I know. But I wish you'd go. Your mother would be pleased.'

'Oh, Simon!' There was chiding in her tone for fairly obvious reasons. 'As a matter of fact, Mummy thinks I ought to stay and look after you—'

'*Does* she? Now just you bloody well listen to me!' Shard said energetically and much more loudly than he had intended, 'you're going and that's an order—no more arguments—' He stopped: there had been a click, a sound of finality. She had hung up on him; something she had never done before. Shard's face flamed, his jaw tightened. He didn't like this, but he wasn't going to call back—not just yet anyway. The mind of a detective slid into gear, personal-problemwise: he'd sounded—maybe—

166

more demanding than was his custom with his wife. Her mind could have moved, possibly mother-in-law aided, along the wrong lines: another woman around and a clear field wanted. If so, that was more stupid than he would have thought possible: in Shard's job, if you were bird-minded, you didn't need to use the home base. The opportunities, provided you kept your official nose clean, were legion and varied and dead easy. Shard happened to be in love with his wife so he'd never bothered. He forced Beth from his mind, not without difficulty, conscious of a little red fury that, all unknowing, she had landed him with a home problem just when London could go sky-high at virtually a moment's notice. His mind was progressing beyond Beth when there was a tap on his door.

He called, 'Come in.'

He had a surprise: it was Elsie, the lady of easy virtue from the next floor up. Perfume swept ahead of her, a first-rate advert for such as liked it. 'I'm ever so sorry to bother you, Mr Sams,' she said, using his philatelic name.

'Don't mention it,' he said politely. 'You're on the go early, aren't you?'

'What d'you mean, on the go?' She giggled.

'Oh, never mind. Are you starting a stamp collection?'

'Not exactly. A friend was asking after you—'

'A friend—of mine?'

'A client. He said he had something you might be interested in.'

'Ah! What, and who, Elsie?'

'I don't know what. He just said like, to tell you, that's all. I don't know his name either, not really. I just know him as Whopper, and—'

'Which?'

'Whopper,' she said, 'and if you like I'll tell you why—'

'Don't bother, I'll guess. Where does Whopper hang out?' That was a mistake: Elsie hooted. *'Live,'* Shard said with asperity. She gave him an address in Tottenham Court Road. He thanked her and sent her off: her perfume stayed behind remindingly. His office ponged like a barber's shop. He sat back in his chair, tapping his fingers thoughtfully on his desk. Whatever their names or their out-of-business-hours desires and habitats, men didn't pass messages just for the fun of it. Somehow that message hadn't had the sound of emanating from a man who wanted to show off his stamp collection. Shard got up, locked his office, clattered down the stairs and walked through rapidly to Tottenham Court Road. He found the number: it was, interestingly, a porn shop; he went in. It was empty inside, a vacuum that was filled upon the tinkle of a bell set off by his entry. From a curtained doorway behind a counter a small man appeared, bright-eyed, perky, with fair wispy hair.

168

'Yes, can I help you, sir?'

Shard said, 'I'd like a word with someone they call Whopper.'

'Ah, yes.' The man coughed, clearing his throat. 'Come inside if you will.' He turned away.

'Just a moment,' Shard said. His right hand, reaching left, was inside his jacket. 'I'd sooner talk here. No offence ... but just go and tell Whopper that, will you?'

'Oh, but I'm Whopper, Whopper Thurgood.'

'I see.' Surprise, surprise! 'Then I think you'll know who I am. Name of Sams. You had something to show me.'

'Tell, actually. Just tell.' Mr Thurgood looked and sounded nervous. 'I'd much rather talk in the back, Mr Shard.'

Shard kept his face blank: it had been likely that his cover had blown after Terry's earlier swoop around his premises, but it was still a shock to hear his name on this man's lips. He said, 'You'll do your talking right here and you'd better make it fast.'

The little man hummed and ha-ed for a few uncertain moments, then climbed down ungraciously. 'All right, if you insist. It's about a man who's been killed up north.'

'York?'

'I see you understand, Mr Shard. In the same line of business, me and him.'

'So?'

'Things travel. Word of mouth—you know.'

'In the porn business?'

'Why not? We're a fraternity, close knit. We have to be, keeping inside the law—'

'Just.'

'Oh dear, Mr Shard, a miss is as good as a mile, you know!' Thurgood sniffed and looked hurt. 'We're like a club, in a way.'

'A club that's told you who I am, and where to find me? A word of explanation, Mr Thurgood, if you please—now.'

'But of course.' Thurgood cleared his throat again: there was something in his eye, something Shard didn't take to, something that warned him that Whopper Thurgood was seeing behind him and experiencing some relief in what he saw . . . Shard swung round just as the doorbell gave another tinkle. He was a fraction too late. Two men had entered, two tall men, two tall men from the Middle East, with guns.

One of them split his dark face into a gleaming, toothy smile beneath a hanging moustache. 'Into the back, please, Mr Shard,' he said.

CHAPTER TWELVE

The room at the back of the shop was stacked high with magazines and books in transparent plastic covers. Shard glanced at them: innocuous on the outside in accordance with the Longford–Whitehouse laws, but inside they wouldn't pass, for instance, the Japanese censorship until customs had been busy on the pubic regions with their black-out pens. It took all sorts, Shard thought.

'Right through, Mr Shard. Out to the back door.'

'We're not stopping?'

'I don't trust policemen. You could have left word where you were going.'

Shard moved on ahead of the guns, out into a passage, out into a side street through a paint-peeled door. Behind came Thurgood, who had apparently shut his shop. As they emerged into the street, the gun-pressure came off Shard's back, but he knew the ropes: in pockets, those guns could still kill. He was close-herded towards an elderly Austin 1100, four door, white with black trim: somehow it failed to look the part, no doubt with prudent intent. Shard was pushed in, with both armed men in the back with him, and Thurgood up front. Another Arabic tough drove. To orders this man took the 1100 into Tottenham Court Road, past a uniformed copper engaged in chiding conversation with a youth on a bicycle: Shard hated seeing the friendly blue fade away behind. But the orders had been, just drive around: from this Shard drew a trace of comfort. The intent was not, it seemed, a snatch—or anyway, not just yet.

The man beside him said, 'Now we talk, and you listen.'

'I listen? You don't want to know anything?'

A laugh: 'We know it all, Detective Chief Superintendent Shard of the Security Service. All your precautions are an open book. The police, the army explosives experts, the night patrols in the tube tunnels—your own visit last night! Yes, we know it all. You have done what you could do. It is not much.'

'But correctly aimed?'

'Correctly aimed, yes. In a broad sense. The whole network is our playground—'

'And more precisely?'

'I have said all I shall say. You have a wide area to cover—around 250 route miles with very many stations. Keep it up, although you cannot win!'

'You sound confident.'

'We are very confident, Shard. Now if you will listen, you may begin to appreciate why.' The Arab paused, looking for a moment at the passing scene, at crowding traffic and bustling

172

pedestrians, workaday London that didn't
know it was so close to disaster and to that
disaster's architects: all it needed, Shard
thought, was some ordinary copper to decide
the 1100's tyres needed a check for tread...
The man beside him went on with his spiel. He
said, 'We have a demand to make.'

'You have?'

'Does this surprise you?'

Shard said, 'I was beginning to wonder.
There's usually something, isn't there?'

'Usually, yes.'

Shard looked sideways into the dark eyes,
eyes that seemed to mock, to be amused. He
said, 'Well, go on, let's have it. Who have we in
custody that you want?'

'You can think of nobody?'

'No.'

The man laughed. 'Neither can I! No, it is
not that, Mr Shard. It is not so simple, so
straightforward ... so easy for you to deal with,
to negotiate over, to perhaps double-deal in
such a way that you can beat us. Do you
understand?'

'Not really. You'll have to be more explicit.'

'I shall be.' The Arab leaned closer. Hot
breath flowed over Shard. 'First let me tell you
this: you have met ... our leader. You have met
others—a handful. But we are many more, Mr
Shard, so very many more than you will
believe, I think! You will find out—and in the

173

meantime you would do well to have a little belief in what I say: that we are strong in numbers. It is important that you should believe this.'

'Important to me—or to you?'

The eyes gleamed. 'Perhaps to both. But now here is the point of what I have to tell you: your underground network, Mr Shard, is to be used to assist us in a certain endeavour . . . to attain a specific object. At this moment I can add little, except—'

'We'll have to know more than that.'

'Before you can bargain?' There was amusement in the voice. '*We* shall not bargain, so—'

'Neither will we. I didn't mean that. I meant, before we can take you seriously, we'll have to know the facts.'

The Arab nodded. 'I see. Perhaps I may remind you, Mr Shard, of some of your British history. Back in the early years of the eighteenth century, a certain company was formed, known as the South Sea Company—'

'The South Sea Bubble—yes, I remember. So?'

'This company . . . it was formed, according to its articles of association, to pursue a purpose the nature of which, I quote, "shall be hereinafter divulged".' The voice grew softer, still with its undercurrent of high amusement. 'This applies to us, Mr Shard. Our purposes will be hereinafter divulged. I would add something else: the watch has not yet been wound up, the mainspring not yet tightened. In short, the—'

'In short, you're not ready yet?'

'True. But only for this reason: our objective ... the thing that will start the action ... this has not yet materialised. When it does, you will not need us to tell you.' Once again the gun nudged harder into Shard's side. 'No questions. I say no more. You must wait now. There is only one thing further before I let you go free, Mr Shard.'

'And that is?'

'We want extra assurance. We want a certain person to be present in the underground system at a time and place that is also to be hereinafter divulged. That person is your chief of security, a Mr Hedge.'

*   *   *

The 1100 had stopped soon after this extraordinary announcement, pulling briefly up alongside a line of parked cars in a road near Regent's Park: Shard was ordered out and at once the car was driven off, disappearing into the traffic. For what it was worth, Shard had the registration number: for his money, the car would have been nicked, would now be quickly abandoned. He was still astonished at the

175

effrontery no less than at the efficiency of an organisation that had dug Hedge out from his nicely classified cover—or almost. A Mr Hedge! They had not, it seemed, arrived at his actual name—which small inaccuracy showed that at least some security remained unblown. What remained of Shard's reaction was sheer mirth: poor Hedge, now regarded by the opposition as that very chief of security for whom he was supposed to be the screen or hedge, was about to do his nut.

He did: back to cloak-and-dagger, Shard and Hedge had a casual meeting in the National Gallery, that crowded, anonymous place of wondering eyes and murmuring adulatory voices. Beneath a splendid nude Hedge went from pink to purple, gasping for breath.

'*Me?*'

'You, Mr Hedge.'

Hedge didn't even notice the cruel Mister. 'How did they find out about me, for God's sake?'

Shard shrugged.

'Anyway, I'm not the you-know-what.' The voice brightened. 'It's not *me* they want—'

'They said they did. By phoney name, Hedge.'

'But I say again, I'm not—'

'All right, all right. Point taken! The thing is, they appear to think you *are*.'

'Didn't you say I wasn't?' Angry eyes stared:

it was like a loudly sounding cry.

Shard said reproachfully, 'Hedge, Hedge! How could I do that?'

Hedge fumed frustratedly: he blew his nose and there was a shake in his fingers, very noticeably: fear was striking home. Shard moved him on: they had lingered long enough by the nude, Hedge was beginning to look like a dirty old man. They paused again, more appropriately perhaps, near scenes of battle and gory horses. Londoners gazed with them, plus foreigners: all sorts and all ages, respectfully admiring the past. Hedge said suddenly, 'Well, they're going to be disappointed. I'm not going! D'you hear?'

'Yes. It's understandable, of course. And I doubt if anyone can make you.'

'I don't care for the way you said that, Shard.'

'Oh? I'm sorry,' Shard said politely. 'It just crossed my mind that it might be wise to co-operate . . . in the interest of the many, you see.'

'Put my life at risk?' Hedge's voice was an angry hiss.

'I'll be taking care of that, Hedge.'

The answer was a snort: Shard grinned inwardly. Hedge didn't say any more, he was too occupied with his thoughts. Pregnant with their combined cerebrations they stole around the National Gallery, Hedge seeing nothing but a coffin filled with fragments, ignoring the masters. They circled back to the entrance and Hedge retrieving his umbrella from the custodian, marched down the steps with Shard, shaking like a leaf now. In Trafalgar Square Shard risked a question: 'Well, Hedge?'

'I told you I'm not going.'

'But you *are* going to report this to the chief—aren't you?'

'Yes!'

They walked on. The silence was not a companionable one. Shard said cheerfully, 'Well, perhaps the chief'll go instead, Hedge.'

'How I detest your stupid jokes. Kindly be serious, Shard. This . . . *thing* that will start the action—that was what you said they said, wasn't it? Have you any ideas?' Hedge, as a few drops of rain started to fall on London, hoisted his umbrella. 'I must confess *I* haven't any.'

'Nor me. It'll be a case of watching out, that's all.'

'A kind of spot the ball contest!'

'You could say that. But when it does come, it's going to be recognisably big. They're not, as the Americans say, in this for peanuts.'

'Quite.' Hedge brooded on, circling Nelson's Column down towards Whitehall, then asked, 'When are you going underground?'

'I'm not sure—now—that I am. Not yet.'

Hedge seemed put out. 'Why the change of mind?'

'Just a hunch. I like to keep flexible.'

'Oh. This hunch ... what is it, Shard?'

'*Just* a hunch—no more.' Shard sighed. 'All right, if you insist—you're the boss. Yesterday I talked of working from the inside out. I've a funny feeling these people mean to work from the outside in. Do you get me, Hedge?'

'No, I don't.'

'I'm not entirely sure I get myself either. But I'm going to wait, and watch, a little longer—'

'The deadline's only three days off—'

'I know, I know. Not to worry too much! We're going to get warning now. Patience, Hedge! And for now, goodbye. I have work to do, people to see.' And so have you, Shard thought as Hedge proceeded across the junction and down Whitehall beneath his spread umbrella. Shard had an idea the FO's Head of Security might expect a degree of co-operation from his Hedge. Hedge was, after all, the screen—and could scarcely expect not to act as such when faced with the supreme moment, the whole *raison d'être*, as it were, of his screendom!

CHAPTER THIRTEEN

Hedge's trumpeted Press clamp-down had failed to work: the early editions of the London evenings had the full story, plus em-

179

bellishments, of the killings in the York intensive care unit: the prime victim, the newspapers said, was a man who had been helping the police with their enquiries. There was an insinuation, however nicely put, that methods used during the 'helping' had contributed to the heart attack that had put the man in hospital. Although he was not named, this was a clear reference to Simon Shard and it made him seethe with a terrible hatred for crime reporters. As ever, they seemed more inclined to impugn a hard-working police force than to inveigh against ruthless killers. Not that there wasn't a degree of inveighing as well; but even this had been neatly turned against the police: how had it been possible for anything like this to take place within the precincts of a hospital where a Detective Constable had been on continuous guard? Worse: the keen amateurs of the Press had been busy, noses fast to the ground. Somewhere, somehow, said the reports, national security was involved: there was a big stick around and it behoved authority to break it across its knee. Dearly Shard would have liked to know where this leak had occurred. And Hedge was going to break a blood-vessel.

Shard did his newspaper reading sitting in an unobtrusive car provided by the Department— during his earlier talk with Hedge he had fixed this, and the response had been nicely immediate: an incoming call to Seddon's Way had announced a Rover 2200 waiting for him whenever he cared to collect. Shard had let it wait a while, until certain reports had reached him from the Yard, mainly negative in the event, pointing the way nowhere: the Austin 1100, as expected, had been stolen that very morning from Gunterstone Road in West Kensington and word of this loss had not reached the Yard's Stolen and Suspect Vehicle index until after its subsequent abandonment near King's Cross railway station. Whopper Thurgood's premises had been done over by the Special Branch, but there was no sign of Thurgood and the only positive result had been a pending porn charge and, *ipso facto*, a lot more porn magazines. But one thing more: the name of a friend of Thurgood's, a name well known to Shard, which accounted for Shard's current activity. Of Nadia Nazarrazeen, of her staunch retinue, no hint. The whole lot had gone underground: at this thought, Shard gave a very hollow laugh. He looked at his watch: his contact was late. Irritably, anxiously, he drummed his fingers on the steering-wheel, then flicked on the car radio for some soothing background music. Pop, however, exacerbated rather than soothed. Shard lost Radio One, got the news headlines on another channel. Much as usual, never any happy news: there was another miners' pay claim coming up, inflation was running at 22 percent, the balance of payments was worse than ever, there had been another hijack, a British VC10 this time, at Athens.

Hijack?

Shard listened intently: anything, almost, could be the triggerpoint. But, he fancied, not this: the hijackers' demands were specific and didn't concern Britain. They wanted two gunmen imprisoned in Greece, two members of the Palestine Liberation movement. They would probably, Shard thought with anger, get them. And thus world authority gradually was eroded . . .

Like now? Shard broke out in a cold sweat: what did the bastards want? Surely, not just Hedge? Sympathy for Hedge came in a sudden wave: half the time Hedge was a bastard too, but this time he was in a real spot. Shard reached out and switched the radio off. A few moments later his contact showed: a tall, thin man in a fawn raincoat, knee length, moving fast through the crowds, eyes watchful. Meeting his glance, Shard lifted a hand and reached to open the passenger door.

The man got in, puffing and wheezing.

'Sorry I'm late. Had a spot of bother.'

'Coppers?'

'Not the coppers, no, the wife.'

'Don't we all.'

The man looked sideways. 'You too, Mr Shard?'

Shard stifled a sigh: Beth, and Mrs Micklam, were still in Ealing, couldn't be shifted. He said, 'I haven't much time. We'll get down to business.'

'What d'you want, Mr Shard?'

Shard said, 'We share an interest: porn.'

'Eh?'

'Just currently, for my part.'

The thin man giggled, an unpleasant sound, high-pitched like a woman. 'Trouble an' strife away, want a genuine inflatable bed-mate, all parts guaranteed to—'

'Shut up, Puckle, or I'll throw you out, no deal. This is serious. It concerns a man called Whopper Thurgood—whom I happen to have discovered is a friend of yours—'

'I know him.'

'Supply him, do you?'

Puckle said, 'Now look, Mr Shard, I'm not—'

'All right, I won't press you towards self-incrimination, but you know as well as I do, this is off the record. So cough as much as you can, understand?'

'What's in it for me?'

'The cash won't interest a porn merchant, and you know that too. I'm not saying more than that, but I'm sure you get the drift, right?'

'You'd pull me in?'

Shard laughed, quietly threatening. 'We both

know the facts of life, don't we? It's not strictly my patch, but I get around, get to know things. Yes, I'd pull you in, so bloody fast your backside wouldn't be seen for dust. Porn, poncing, male prostitution—you name it, the court'll send you down for it.'

Puckle's face was sour. 'Scratch a copper and you find a—'

'That, we'll take as read. Start coughing, Puckle.'

'About what?'

'Whopper Thurgood, his business, his friends—social and trade—his contacts, especially recent ones—'

'I supply him, I don't bloody share his pad—'

'You're a personal friend. I want the lot, and I mean the lot. Any recent changes . . . anything that's been on his mind, journeys he's made, people who've visited . . . anything at all, everything. I want Thurgood to be an open book, and after you've coughed, I want you to keep your trap shut tight. Don't even breathe if you can avoid it. Is all this clearly understood?'

'It's a bit much!' Puckle was indignant. 'I can't—'

'If you fail me, I'll bring joy to the heart of a certain Detective Chief Superintendent at New Scotland Yard, a friend of mine . . . he already has the charges typed, and he can't wait. You'll be ripped apart, no chance. You'll be out of circulation for years, and you know as well as I do, ponces always get a rough ride from the other cons.' Shard paused. 'As a matter of fact—this is a funny thing, Puckle—I said something rather similar to someone else. Only yesterday, it was. In York.'

He waited, not seeming to watch Puckle's face. In any case it remained blank, though Shard believed he sensed a stiffening of the body alongside him. He went on, 'That man's dead now. I expect you've read about it.' He thrust his newspaper at Puckle. 'Front page stuff. Name of Larger, porn merchant in a nice way of business.'

Puckle whistled. 'Dead! In bloody hospital!'

'It happens, but not normally this way. You didn't know?'

'No. Hadn't seen the paper yet.'

Shard said, 'You're a liar, Puckle. Get a grip on the facts. Larger's dead, Thurgood's vanished. You're a link of a sort—'

'Ah—of a sort, maybe.'

'Don't bank on the tenuousness of that link. Just take a look at the facts. You don't want to be murdered, or even to risk the possibility. So start talking.'

★   ★   ★

At the far end of the station buffet at Victoria, Shard drank a large Scotch and talked quietly to Assistant Commissioner Hesseltine. 'We sweated it out together,' he said. 'I got Puckle in a tizzy. He's not a strong-minded man. So far as I can see, there's absolutely no reason why anyone should want to kill him—or anyway, there *wasn't*—but currently he's a very convinced man in fear of imminent murder.'

'Does this help—and if so, how?'

'Shard grinned. 'Oh, it helps! I've promised him protection, a shield against murder—'

'Does he believe in us that much?'

'Probably not, but he sees it as his only hope—especially since he talked.' Shard toyed with his glass, now empty. 'Larger and Thurgood were in contact, two or three times over the last couple of weeks. And a woman came to see Thurgood one night, when Puckle happened to be delivering stock unexpectedly.'

Their eyes met: Hesseltine's eyebrows were lifted. Shard nodded his answer. 'As ever was,' he said, 'by Puckle's description. And of course she knows of Puckle's existence now if she didn't before. That could be bad for Puckle—at any rate, he now believes it could.'

'Under the influence of Shard?'

Again Shard nodded. 'Dead right, sir. I told you, he's a weak man, very susceptible to suggestion.'

'So?'

'So I'm setting him up. I'm dropping word into the grapevine that he's been questioned along relevant lines—'

186

'But will they care? Does it matter now?'

'You mean, seeing they've approached me direct?'

'Yes. Hasn't Puckle been by-passed?'

Shard shrugged. 'It's possible, I agree. But it's worth a shot. They won't know just how much he picked up from Thurgood, even maybe from Larger. They won't be sure how much he's said, how much he hasn't. There's a whole lot of need for secrecy still, from their angle—those Arabs only told me as much as I had to know.'

'Yes, true.' Hesseltine frowned, lit a cigarette, blew smoke thoughtfully over Shard's head. 'So they go out to get him—you hope! How's he taking that?'

'He doesn't know he's being set up, exactly,' Shard said. 'I didn't go into that bit, the *deliberate* bit.'

'It's dirty, Simon.'

'Very dirty. I don't pretend to like it any more than you. But this thing has to be beaten.'

'Well, you don't belong to me any more, so it's not for me to give orders. You'll have to make your own decisions. What about Hedge?'

Shard looked down again at his empty glass. 'Hedge has other things on his mind just now. I haven't had an opportunity of telling him. I'm discussing it with you instead, sir.'

'Why?'

Shard grinned. 'Question of availability, and

I wanted to clear my own mind. Also something else.'

'I thought there might be! Well?'

'Obviously, I'll be watching Puckle like a hawk—this, he'll be expecting as part of the protection promise. I want assistance.'

Hesseltine objected. 'I'm Yard, you're FO. Use your own mob, Simon.'

Shard shook his head. 'Again, there's a question of availability. I have a lot of men on tube duty and I have a sick list—injuries, two of my best DSs. And I've not been long with the FO, as you know, sir. I still tend to work best on this sort of job with men I've known from the beat up. Will you bear with me, just this time?'

Hesseltine blew out a long breath, irritably. 'Thin end of the wedge, and ultimately all for your horrible master! Who d'you want?'

'Thanks,' Shard said gratefully. 'I'd like Detective Sergeants Williams and Kenwood. No personal contact for now. I'd like them to check in on the security line to my office.'

*   *   *

Hedge, as it transpired later, had indeed had a bad time. His report to the Head of Security had been made with trepidation and yet with hope. And with a deprecating laugh, as though they had the sheerest lunacy to deal with.

'The most extraordinary effrontery, sir!'

Silver-haired elegance, urbanity, excellent tailoring that made the most of a well-kept waistline, sat easily in a luxurious armchair: easily and, Hedge thought with sudden disloyalty, *safely*. And all because of a mistake! With rising anger at being forced to make the running himself, Hedge underlined the mistake angle: 'Especially since it appears it's you they want, sir.'

'Yes...'

'They've had too much encouragement in the past, of course.'

The elegant face looked vague: light blue eyes, shrewd eyes, focused on Hedge. 'H'm?'

'They mustn't have it this time, sir.'

A shrug: 'Well, I think it rather depends on what it is they're proposing to put London at risk *for*, don't you? We don't know yet what that is. We must wait and see, my dear fellow.'

'But really—'

'You know as well as I do, these people have to be kid-gloved up to a point. The days of gunboat diplomacy are over—even in police terms. Regrettable, but true, and we must face it. The authority of force has already passed to the other side. I'm sure you understand that, don't you?'

Hedge glowered, the pink of his face deepening. 'So you want us to play along with them, sir. Is that it?'

'Come, come—not all along the line! But up to a point, certainly. We have no alternative. We'll talk again, of course, as soon as they've been in contact—that'll be the time for decision. In the meantime, I'd be obliged if you'd hold yourself in readiness, Hedge.'

'Readiness, sir?' Hedge's jaw dropped. 'Do I take it you mean to go along with this ridiculous demand, then?'

The Head of Security spread his hands. 'Must I make all my points over again? We must be seen to be willing to co-operate for quite some of the way. This could involve even an actual, physical hand-over, but have no fear. We shall not sacrifice you.'

'How do you ensure that?' Hedge burst out. 'How *can* you be so sure? And remember it's you they want—not me. What happens when they find out?'

'They mustn't find out, my dear chap. They mustn't! You're my Hedge. I rely on you to maintain a very close cover of me.' There was a dismissive wave: Hedge left the presence, feeling expendable and mutinous. Feeling also that the chief was committing an error of monumental proportions ... but there had to be a better word than monumental! Hedge shivered, fear striking deep. His job it was to inspire confidence in his agents, his admin staff, his field men, his Shards: now he had to inspire confidence in his own mind, for it was his own organisation that would have to be his last safeguard. Walking back along the stately corridors of tradition, the corridors once trodden by British aristocrats against whom no damned terrorist would have dared raise a finger—times long ago—Hedge felt cold and already forgotten, a man doomed to oblivion in death, for however nobly he might die if it should come to that, the only memory permitted to a dead Hedge was a withering one, a thing of no overt honour.

CHAPTER FOURTEEN

Tom Casey, Father Donnellan, the dropout Nose, Larger, Nadia Nazarrazeen, the eager lover carved and dropped down the Buttertubs by far-off lonely Swaledale ... none of them had revealed quite enough. The police in Yorkshire had retrieved that last body from its deep pit and it hadn't been worth the effort, the risk to good coppers going down on ropes: there was no information about him obtainable anywhere. He had come in anonymously from some Middle Eastern country and he had exited this life in an eroded limestone shaft and that was that. It was still, as the Head of Security had told Hedge, a matter of waiting: as ever, terrorism held the initiative. Despondently

Shard, his men now strategically placed to keep discreet observation on Puckle's flat in Half Moon Street off Piccadilly, reviewed the known facts, sitting in his car in radio contact a few streets away—like everybody else, waiting. His review of the facts took him no time at all: his mind moved on, restlessly, surveying the precautions taken, the deployment of forces, the watch on the network of tunnels—and all the things that couldn't be protected except by a total excision of the threat: the intricacies of electric cables, the maze of pipes carrying gas, the great channels of fresh water and London sewage, to say nothing of the foundations of buildings, so many of them close enough to the river sections that Shard considered the most likely target area: the Festival Hall, the Shell building, Whitehall Court, the Houses of Parliament themselves, just to name the biggest.

The call, coming in on his radio, using his personal call sign, though half expected and eagerly awaited, made him jump: and it wasn't the one he'd hoped for, the one that would have told him of movement around the Puckle pad.

Hedge.

'S 1 to S 2, over.'

'S 2 answering. What is it now? Over.'

Hedge's voice came thinly but with urgency. 'Report in person. Now. No arguments, this is vital and can't be said *en clair*. Do not, repeat not, call me back.'

Click: Hedge went off. Shard swore lurid oaths and blasphemies as, by obeying Hedge, he withdrew back-up support from his watchful DCs under Detective Sergeant Kenwood. Report in person, in the absence of any precise instruction, meant the Foreign Office, which was normally alien to Hedge's cloak-and-dagger outlook: just how vital, just how secret, was this? Shard drove fast, savagely, from his temporary resting-place into Piccadilly. Not all that secret, it seemed! Shard roared along Piccadilly: Pandas prowled, plus the odd beat man, keeping eyes on wandering hippies, junkies clustering around the Circus, the general sordidness of the West End at night. Haymarket, Trafalgar Square, Whitehall, Foreign Office, Hedge. Dimly silent-hourly-lit corridors led to Hedge, sitting at his desk and listening to one of his telephones.

Their eyes met: Hedge waved towards a chair and Shard sat down, still feeling angry. Hedge finished his conversation, put down the handset, and lost no time.

'Shard, I said this was urgent and it is. I've had news of something big that could be the target for attack—'

'You mean the *reason* for attack, don't you, Hedge?'

'Yes, yes. Don't split hairs. Listen.' Hedge leaned across the desk, heavy and flabby-faced

193

but serious. 'Two men are flying into Heathrow from the Lebanon tomorrow evening. We've only just been warned by our Embassy in Beirut—they've only just been given the tip themselves. These birds are flying in with an American escort, under arrest—'

'*American*, Hedge?'

'American.' Hedge was in a state of controlled fury. 'You'd think we'd have been informed—we're allies, after all. But no, not a word. They'll touch down in a British Airways VC 10 at five thirty-five for onward flight to Kennedy via TWA. So for two hours, a little over, they'll be in Britain. Got that so far?'

'Not difficult. And I don't like it. What's the hook-up, Hedge?'

'Also not difficult. These men are wanted very badly in the States—we want them too, but as of now they're U.S. property. Now, they were arrested by CIA agents before they could fly to Venezuela, which is where they want to go—I'll come back to that in a moment. It so happens there's a TWA flight from Heathrow to Maracaibo scheduled for just after the Kennedy flight—'

'And you think these birds'll want to be on it? Who are they, Hedge?'

Hedge said ominously, 'Fatah al Ahmedi and Khaled ben Suli.'

'Both Black September.'

'Right! Hijacks in Kuwait, at Kennedy—

194

Heathrow—Amsterdam—only … bomb outrages too numerous to specify … kidnaps, murders ditto. I needn't go on—you know them.'

'And this time?'

Hedge stared, mopped at his face: his eyes looked wild, and no wonder, with his personal involvement. 'This time?' he repeated.

'You said, Venezuela. What did they mean to do there?'

Hedge mopped again. 'Venezuela … it's been known for some while that there's to be a top-level conference there. All the terrorist brass—you know the kind of thing, brewing up world revolution—these two men are the lynch-pins of the Executive. America—the President himself was determined they shouldn't make it, quite apart from the fact of the charges pending in the States. Our proper attitude is, of course, quite clear: we give the escort every facility and we see the men are put aboard the TWA for Kennedy.' Hedge gestured in the air. 'If we don't—if this is the objective of the threat to London, d'you see—well, there'll be all kinds of pressures from Washington—'

'But in fact the threat itself is the principal one,' Shard broke in. Back in that 1100, the man had said positively enough that there was nobody they wanted out of custody, but within the context of that conversation British gaol custody could have been the point of reference;

195

there didn't have to be any contradiction. 'If we're right, Hedge, why not warn the Americans off, order the VC 10 to land somewhere else?'

He sat down; Hesseltine nodded. 'Take due note, at a high level. The view is that it wouldn't help, nor would it help to deny the Americans use of a British flight, tell them to make other arrangements—'

'Why can't they use a military aircraft, Hedge?'

'In point of fact, I dare say they can. But we're still stuck with it in the official view—in my view too.' Hedge waved a finger in Shard's face. 'Unless those terrorists are given clearance for a flight to Maracaibo from *anywhere in the world*, London goes up. Assuming we've made the right deductions initially, it seems obvious. They must always have considered our possible reaction when we ticked over, and they must have known we'd get the word in time to order a deviation. But they chose London.'

'So, in the event of a deviation, they'll rely on pressure-waves emanating from Whitehall?'

'Of course! We still have a few friends left, nations who'll spare a thought for London. That's what these people would bank on. I say again, unless we co-operate London goes up.' Hedge shivered suddenly. 'And so do I!'

'You, Hedge? You're going in as demanded?'

Hedge nodded wordlessly.

'You have guts, Hedge.'

'I'm under orders. I sometimes think my master has no feelings.'

'You're still a brave man.'

Hedge seemed to crumple: his head went down in his hands. 'I haven't any option ... I'd be dropped like a hot potato. I'm not a man of real means, Shard, not with all this bloody socialism from both parties. I can't exist on my pension ... and I detest poverty, it's the ultimate horror so far as I'm concerned.' He lifted his head, stared unseeingly at Shard, then seemed to stiffen himself. 'Besides, there's the national interest.'

'Of course. Not to worry, though—we'll get you out.'

Hedge glowered. 'You never liked me, did you, Shard.'

Shard felt jolted, and suddenly immensely sorry. He said, 'No, that's not true, we haven't made a bad team. In any case, that doesn't come into it. You have my absolute assurance that I'll get you out.'

'There's many a slip.'

'Sure. But we're throwing in all we've got. I say again, don't worry.' Shard paused. Things had to be settled now. 'When d'you go, and how?' It sounded horribly like a trip to Majorca.

Hedge said, 'I don't know, they haven't

contacted yet. If I'm right, they'll do so at any moment.'

'Here, by telephone?'

'I don't know. What do you think?'

'Could be *my* office, I suppose—'

'Yes.' Hedge pounced on that. 'You're their contact man. You'd better get over there, Shard, quick as you can—'

'I'm on a job, an important one. You know that, Hedge.'

'This takes priority. I'm sorry. Don't you see, it's going to be the contact? As a matter of fact, I think I'll come with you.'

'Look here—'

'I suppose it wouldn't help to have a tap?'

Shard said impatiently, 'You know it wouldn't. They'll use a call-box and they'll make it quick, won't they?'

'Yes, I suppose so.' Hedge looked and sounded sick, as though he could make no further effort but could only wait around to be placed in the Black September or whatever other net it might be with murderers and hijackers and bomb-throwers as his last companionship upon earth. Shard felt sorrier and sorrier: for much of the time past Hedge had been a self-seeking pink bastard, but he was facing this well enough. Presumably he was wanted as extra cover, and would be held until the terrorists reached Maracaibo . . .

Shard got to his feet. 'If we're going, let's go.'

'Yes, yes . . .' They went down to Shard's car.

As they went Hedge started on something else: 'Shard, I've had the Home Office on the line. Some highly placed doctor ... they've dug up Weil's Disease.'

Shard stared. 'Come again?'

'During the war a bomb penetrated the subways at Tooting and hit a train. The guard, or maybe it was the driver—he managed to get out and walk back along the tunnel, up to his shoulders in water. He was shaken up, but otherwise seemed all right.' Hedge paused and blew his nose. 'A couple of days later he was dead.'

'How?'

'I told you. Weil's Disease.'

'Which is?'

'A particularly nasty form of jaundice, contracted through water infected by rats' faeces.'

Shard shook his head in wonder and said, 'Gamma rays, Hedge!'

'What?'

'Aren't we facing something rather bigger than jaundice, however nasty?'

Dully Hedge nodded. 'Yes, I suppose so, but it's an extra worry, isn't it?' He didn't say anything further. Once in the Rover, they sat in silence. Shard thought about rat excreta: gamma rays or not, it was certainly another hazard. Hedge hadn't said whether that unfortunate tube man had waded through the outflow of a broken sewer or of a fresh-water main; but by the time the mix-up came, it wouldn't be important, sewers and fresh water would be all one and this Weil's Disease might be everywhere. And if there was one disease, there could presumably be others...

Shard let himself into his office, flicked on the lights, and went across to the cupboard where he kept whisky. He lifted an eyebrow at Hedge.

Hedge nodded. 'Thank you.'

Shard poured neat measures, took his in one quick fling down his throat. He lit a cigarette, sat at his desk, shoulders hunched, starting the waiting game again. Hedge's imaginings could be all to hell, however logical they might sound. Hedge, in the meantime, looked as though his imagination was running riot. In the event no telephone call came; but after some half an hour of monosyllabic conversation with Hedge, Shard's personal transceiver bleeped him from his pocket and he brought it out. It was Kenwood calling. 'Go ahead,' Shard said.

'Chummy has visitors: one woman, two men.'

Shard's knuckles whitened: Nadia Nazarrazeen? He said, 'This woman: check identity?'

Kenwood's voice came thinly, 'Check!'

'Sure?'

'Sure enough from the description, sir.

Action?'

'If anyone leaves, tail. Short of that, hold it—I'm on my way.' Shard flicked off, shoved the transceiver back into his pocket and met the angry eye of Hedge.

Hedge asked, 'What was all that, then?'

Shard explained. He said, 'I'm going in—you heard. I'd like you to come.'

'But the phone call—'

'It can wait, this can't. They can ring again, can't they?' Shard was checking his gun. 'This is the boss woman moving in. You may not need to be handed over—it could mean you'll live, Hedge! Isn't that a nice thought?' He gave a hard grin. 'It's time you saw a little field work for yourself, just in case!'

Hedge's mouth opened for another protest, but Shard hustled him towards the door.

*   *   *

'Kenwood?' Shard kept his voice low: there was silence in Half Moon Street, silence and emptiness and a kind of pregnant ominousness. Walking in past the night-shrouded offices with flats above had been like entering a tomb, the DS in the shadows like some brooding priest.

'Yes, sir.'

'They're still there?'

'Still there, sir.'

'Came by car—did they?'

201

'Jaguar XJ12, black. Dropped them and went on.' Detective Sergeant Kenwood waved a hand, ghost-like. 'Parked round the corner.'

'How about the back of the premises?'

'Two DCs watching, sir.'

'Right, fine. Any lights visible?'

'First floor flat, sir—Puckle's. Window left of the front door.'

'And the front door?'

'Appears to open by remote control on the tenant being called on an intercom system.'

'Right,' Shard said again. 'We're going in, Kenwood. Bring up your front DCs, will you?' He watched while Kenwood stepped into the road, lifted an arm, and stepped back again into the shadows. Four figures closed in, joining Shard and Kenwood. Shard said, 'Extreme care, all of you. They may be expecting us. I'll approach the front door alone. I want the rest of you round the corner in Piccadilly. Sergeant Kenwood will watch for my signal . . . when the door opens, I'll wave. Then you come in fast, but as quietly and unobtrusively as possible. All right?' Shard delayed no longer: as Kenwood sent his DCs off singly into Piccadilly, Shard moved towards the door, taking it slow and casual, climbed the short flight of steps, examined the night-lit bell-pushes, and pressed Puckle's. After an interval, a voice came at Shard, about head height, on the intercom: 'Who is it?'

'Nose,' Shard said in a hoarse voice, half smothered by a coughing attack.

'Nose?'

'From York. It's about Pearson. Something you ought to know, mate.'

Shard waited: they would wonder how Nose had come to know Puckle, but they wouldn't keep him hanging about: Men like Nose, men who smelt of meths and overall rough sleeping, tended to attract attention. A few moments later, with nothing more said, the heavy door clicked open fractionally. Shard gave it a push: the way was wide. Stepping back, he waved, saw the responding shadows move inwards. Holding the door open, he went in with his gun ready. Behind him, Kenwood with his four DCs crowded a narrow hall. Operated from somewhere above, a dim light went on and they saw the stairs at the end of the hall. No stealth now: they ran for the stairs, flat out, Shard in the lead, praying to God that they might dodge the bullets. He was aware as he ran that there had been no mistake in the identification of the woman seen going in: her scent was on the air, fragrant, pervasive reminder of sexuality. So far, this was the only manifestation. Shard reached a landing, saw the door to Puckle's flat, solid wood, white painted. It seemed peaceful, there was even an air of abandonment. Shard went forward, was utterly unprepared for what happened: the door came open suddenly, very suddenly, drawn inwards, and he saw fire, what looked like a flaming bundle of clothing. Held by two tall men, dark-faced and dark haired, the bundle was hurled straight at Shard. Shard went down beneath it, heard the shouts of his men behind him, heard the stutter of an automatic and felt the transmitted thud of bullets into the flaming, stinking bundle. The smell was not new to Shard: burning flesh, plus petrol. He struggled out from under, beating at his own clothing, the stench in his nostrils nauseating. There was another burst of gunfire, returned by the plain-clothes men behind Shard. Bullets whistled past his head, pinging into walls and woodwork: then the door of the flat slammed shut. Shard ran for it, threw his weight against its solidity: it held, locked fast from inside. He looked round, saw that Kenwood was on his feet with one of his DCs. Three others lay sprawled on the stairs, pouring blood. Shard used his transceiver, called the Yard, rapped an urgent appeal for men and ambulances. Then he looked down at the burning corpse.

'Petrol,' he said. 'Puckle. Puckle in petrol . . . poor bastard!'

Kenwood, by the door of the flat, said, 'Inside, sir.' He pointed: smoke was coming round the jamb. 'We'll need the fire brigade. Better tell the Yard.'

'Right. In the meantime, get that door

down.' Shard flicked his radio again. Bullets smashed into the lock, uselessly. There would be bolts ... Kenwood and his remaining DC, plus Shard, turned into battering rams. When one of the panels gave, the result was billowing smoke, thick and acrid, no hope of getting through. Cursing, Shard left Kenwood to take over, and himself went down the stairs at the rush, out to the back of the premises, behind the well of the staircase. A door with glass panels gave exit to a small back yard. Outside, Shard looked up: fire escape. The obvious route out, and unless Kenwood's men had been on the ball, the birds would have flown, over walls and away. Shard ran back through the house into Half Moon Street. Heads were looking out of upper windows, people were starting to fill the street, then Shard heard the police sirens. They came in screaming—patrol cars, ambulances, fire appliances, blue lights flashing like Blackpool in high summer. Shard found a uniformed Chief Inspector, briefly gave him the summary. They were bringing the bodies down when Hedge turned up, unable to remain in the Rover and never mind security.

'Shard! My God! What happened?'

Shard told him, moved aside as sudden stench announced the out-going Puckle. Hedge stared as the charred corpse was borne past to one of the ambulances. 'What's that, for God's sake?'

'A man called Puckle, porn merchant.'

Hedge still stared as though totally fascinated, his face pouring sweat. 'I don't know how you can stand it, Shard, how you have the stomach...' The inward light in his eye said he was thinking of his own future.

'I'm a field man, Hedge. All this ... it's the base of the triangle.'

'Triangle?'

'Of which you're the summit—or just below.'

'It's horrible.' Hedge seemed to give himself a mental shake, stared at the crowds being held back by the police. 'What about the boss woman as you called her?'

'Flown, I'd say.' Shard turned as Detective Sergeant Kenwood came up, blackened with fire and smoke, clothes still smouldering. 'Well?'

'Flat's empty, sir—I went in with a smoke helmet.'

'The back—your men, your DCs?'

'Kenwood lifted his hands, let them fall again. 'I'm sorry, sir. They went up the fire escape when they heard the shooting. They were gunned down ... not killed, but put out of action.'

Sweat streamed down Shard's face. A hard knot of fury swelled inside: his fault—a botched job, and his men the sufferers from something he'd set up himself. A sour sickness rose, but he fought it down. 'The car—the Jag?'

'Still parked, sir. They must have had another available—just in case.'

'So the trail's dead?'

No answer from Kenwood. Shard swung round on Hedge. 'We're doing no good here, you at any rate had better fade. And stand by for a contact.'

'Yes.' Hedge looked ghastly in the flickering blue lights, the yellow floods of the firemen. Shard put a hand on his shoulder and walked with him to a police car. As it happened, the driver was taking a message from the Yard: recognising Shard he said, 'They want a Mr Hedge, sir.'

'That's me,' Hedge said. 'What is it?'

'An urgent call's come into your office, sir. There's a Duty Officer asking for instructions.'

'Tell the caller to ring again in ten minutes,' Hedge said. 'I'm going to my office now. Shard, you'd better come with me.'

'Better still,' Shard said. 'I'll drive you.' With Hedge he ran round the corner into Piccadilly and got into the Rover.

★   ★   ★

In Hedge's office, they waited. Hedge sat slumped in his chair behind his desk, staring at his telephones. He had just his desk light on: the room was mostly in shadow. In the shadows Shard prowled, unable to rest, to relax, tugging

207

hard at a cigarette. All along it had been a kind of failure: so near and yet never quite near enough, and far too many deaths. Any moment now they would steam into the final act, and tomorrow there might be wholesale slaughter in London. As for days past they were as ready as they could be: all police and troops on stand-by, the tube tunnels undergoing full night search. All reports had indicated no explosives, but Shard knew very well that this meant, in fact, no explosives found, which was a different thing. The continuing search was an obvious essential, but Shard reckoned it a waste of time and effort: the explosive potential wouldn't be there yet, it would go down after the first trains started running, when the commuters began to flood the booking halls and the escalators and platforms. Shard, his nerve-endings reacting now, looked at his watch: it was more than ten minutes, the bastards were late, were probably holding off deliberately with intent to rattle even more—or maybe the activities of their brother vandals, the small-scale vandals, had made the finding of another call-box in working order a hard task: they wouldn't be hanging around the one they had made the first call from.

Hedge said, 'God, this can't go on.' His voice shook: Shard knew the hell he was going through. A few seconds after Hedge had spoken his telephone, the ordinary outside line already put through to him by the switchboard, burred, a soft sound but menacing. Shard held his breath, moved swiftly and silently towards the monitor as Hedge lifted his handset.

CHAPTER FIFTEEN

'This is the Foreign Office?'

'Yes.'

'British Security?'

Hedge didn't answer that. He asked, 'Who's calling?'

'I wish to speak,' the voice, a woman's, went on in disregard of the question, 'to Mr Hedge.'

Hedge's face went a shade greyer and his voice grew higher. 'This is Hedge speaking. Who's that?'

'It is not important. This is: you will, I think, know by this time that tomorrow two persons will arrive at Heathrow in transit to Kennedy...' Over the handset, the pleading eyes of Hedge vainly sought Shard's: Shard was listening on the monitor. The theorising had been spot on and now there wasn't long to go. The voice—and Shard had recognised it instantly as being that of Nadia Nazarrazeen— told Hedge in detail all that he knew already. 'If there is any interference with the two men by either the British or the Americans,' the voice

209

said coolly, 'London will suffer—how, you know already, I think. You must not doubt that we shall do as we say, and it will not save London if you should refuse landing facilities to the VC 10 or if the Americans should cut the Heathrow call.' The eyes of Hedge and Shard met for an instant. 'There is one further requirement: the flight to Maracaibo will take off from Heathrow without its passengers, travelling only with its flight-deck crew and one stewardess, and the persons from Beirut.' Just in case, Shard thought, of concealed guns carried by anonymous British or American agents. The voice went on, 'Now we come to your personal part, Mr Hedge. Are you listening?'

Hedge licked his lips, glanced again at Shard's intent face. 'I'm listening,' he said.

'Then go out into Whitehall and walk towards the Houses of Parliament, Mr Hedge, on foot and alone.'

'When?'

'Now. Cross Parliament Street by the subway leading to Bridge Street. You know?'

'Yes.'

'There is a men's lavatory. As you pass it, two men will come out behind you. You will walk straight on through to Bridge Street. The men will remain behind you—they will not harm you in any way if you follow your instructions carefully, Mr Hedge. You will walk along Bridge Street without looking behind you, and you will turn down left before Westminster Bridge and walk along the Embankment, keeping to the left-hand pavement.'

'And then?'

There was a light laugh: Shard could almost smell the perfume. 'Then you will see. For now, that is all.'

Hedge was desperate. 'Wait—' he stopped, with a stupid look on his face: the call had been cut. He stared at Shard, his whole flabby face wobbling. He gasped like a fish. 'I've got to have protection, Shard!'

Shard said, 'You're on your own now, Hedge.'

'For God's sake . . . whose side are you on?'

'I'm facing facts, so must you. Take a grip, Hedge. You have a few minutes . . . I'd suggest you ring the chief.'

'Yes,' Hedge said quickly: there was a look that said he might be given a last-minute reprieve if he rang the chief. 'Yes, that's a good idea.' His fingers shook as he took up his closed line and called the home of the Head of Security. A pause, a drumming of fingers, Hedge whitening fast around the gills . . .

'Hedge, sir. Yes. I'm sorry—it's vital.' Briefly, he passed the gist of the recent call, then listened, going whiter still. The inference was obvious enough to Shard: no reprieve.

Hedge scarcely kept his polite obsequiousness: he almost slammed the instrument down. 'I have to go,' he said to Shard. 'I have to follow instructions precisely and to the letter.' His tone was hopeless, defeated, a bitter echo of the inner knowledge that he was but one life against London's millions, but one life against the forces of international terrorism. It was a grotesquely hard order, vicious in its possible intent: these people just might be satisfied with Hedge alone, who by that token would stand a chance of saving London by his personal sacrifice. Shard, recognising this, also recognised that Hedge's long knowledge of the security services, longer by far than Shard's, told him that expediency was all and that at the ultimate summit crouched the ultimate in bastardy...

Shard dropped him a thin line of hope. He said. 'Not too precisely, Hedge.'

'What?'

'The instructions—not a blind follow. They said, alone. All right, you'll be alone. But you'll have a tail: me.'

'But the chief said—'

'Never mind the chief, Hedge. I'll be behind you.' Shard looked at his watch: time had passed, the hands showed one thirty-five—D Day now, with something around sixteen hours to go. Shard thought, with a shaft of pain, of Beth: no time to ring now, he'd call later if and

212

when the chance came during what was going to be a busy day. 'Whatever the woman said, they'll expect a tail, Hedge—the fact there is one, if they cotton on, won't make it any worse for you—'

'But if they intercept—'

'That'll be just too bad, but I'm not inexperienced, Hedge.'

'No, no, of course not.' Hedge mopped a cold sweat from his face, looked much relieved that he wasn't being totally cast to the lions yet. 'Thank you very much, Shard. I appreciate what you're doing.'

Shard grinned, forebore to say that what he was doing would be in the national, rather than the Hedge interest. He glanced meaningly at Hedge's pansy French clock, and Hedge took the hint. Quaking, he moved to a cupboard and brought out bowler hat and umbrella and thus decently equipped went to the door. He looked back with a silly expression on his face, as though taking a last maudlin leave of something he would never see again. Before moving into the corridor he thought of something else, and paused.

'Shard, my wife.'

'Well?'

'She'll have to know . . .'

Shard said, 'Hedge, you're not going out incognito. They're obviously going to use you as a bargaining counter, aren't they, so—'

'Shard, Shard—she doesn't know I'm *Hedge*!'

Shard felt a little foolish. 'Point taken—I'm sorry. So what d'you want me to do? Blow your security to her?'

'No, no.' Hedge looked terribly irresolute, almost in tears of worry and indecision and an increasing fearfulness. 'Really, I don't know what ... I suppose you could ring her, Shard, and say I've been called away at short notice—Scotland or Northern Ireland—any-where you like. Yes, I think that would do it.' He looked at Shard like a pleading pink dog. 'You will, won't you?'

Shard had a moment of cruelty, but it passed. Beth had had no such consideration shown in her fancied widowhood, but perhaps that was no reason to out-Hedge Hedge. He nodded. 'All right, leave it with me. Now you'd better get going.'

'And you, Shard?'

'I'll go out by another door and kind of outflank the gents. I'll be seeing you, Hedge!'

'I hope so,' Hedge said fervently.

★   ★   ★

Shard contacted a minor diplomat on duty and used his own rank and appointment: for anonymity's sake he took over the diplomat's car, a dark green Triumph, and personally wrenched off the CD plates with the assistance

214

of the diplomat's bag of car tools. He drove out of Downing Street, past the police on guard at Number 10 where lights were burning in a line of upstairs windows, turned left along Whitehall. Looking right as he turned, he failed to see Hedge: no doubt by this time he had already made the gents in the subway. Before Trafalgar Square Shard took a right turn into Whitehall Place, past the Ministry of Defence where more lights were burning: as he drove past, some military brass was being decanted from staff cars: the chief had been busy, no doubt, after the call from Hedge. For all Shard could tell, though Hedge hadn't indicated he was wanted, his security line would be burring away beneath Elsie and her easy virtue in Seddon's Way, though not loudly enough to put her customers off their stroke. Or—a sinking thought—Beth would be answering the home line and getting herself in a panic to be exacerbated by Mrs Micklam ... Shard forced home from his mind with an effort the intensity of which told him he was becoming a worse cop than ever, and drove slow into the bottom end of Northumberland Avenue. He turned left onto the Embankment, drove on for fifty yards, then drifted in to the kerb and stopped. There was no one around, not even a policeman, not even a dropout, meths-filled, looking for a night's shakedown. A wind blew along the silent Thames, cold around Cleopatra's Needle

215

ahead of him, gently rustling the spring leaves on the trees. Shard watched out in his rear-view mirror: after a while something came into sight, a couple, almost wrapped around each other. Then something else, something being pushed. He swivelled, taking a direct and confirmatory look: a brace of London's night workers, street sweepers pushing a mobile dust-bin, a small hand-cart of rubbish. They crossed the road towards the river and began pushing their long-handled brooms along the gutter, dead slow, lethargic, unsupervised. A few minutes later the expected procession came into view, not positively identifiable at that distance, but likely enough: one man with two more behind, around a dozen yards astern.

Shard backed past the end of Northumberland Avenue, turned left into it and then right past Charing Cross underground and into Villiers Street. Parking the Triumph, he slipped silently, shadow-like, into Victoria Embankment Gardens. From the cover of evergreens he watched as the trio came nearer, moving along the pavement on the side away from the river. Closer identification was made: bowler hat and umbrella assisted. Hedge moved past, looking dead scared, no more than six feet away. Behind him the two characters, ex-gents: a decidedly Middle Eastern look, but Shard didn't recognise them as anyone he had encountered in the earlier phases. They all went past peacefully, like a bishop with his attendant acolytes. But they wouldn't, Shard fancied, walk for ever: somewhere, there had to be a vehicle, which meant he had for his part to retain contact with the Triumph. He slid back from the bushes, through the gardens, into the driving seat, turned in Villiers Street and drove back under the railway arch into Northumberland Avenue to left-turn again for the Embankment, the intention being to drive innocently fast towards Waterloo Bridge and then wait once more farther along. But, not for the first time, intent was frustrated by present fact: now you see him, now you don't, Shard thought grimly.

Hey presto and Hedge had gone, vanished. So had the two men from the lavatory. So had the mutually wrapped lovers. Ahead up the road, a tattered figure crossed to lean over and gaze upon the London river. A cop car cruised gently past. On the off-chance, Shard stopped it: result nil. Nothing seen. On the river side the two street sweepers swept mournfully, removing filth from the purlieus of the rich, now and again opening up the hatch in the mobile dustbin to throw in the garnerings.

Shard cursed. On the off-chance he drove ahead, vainly looking left. He retraced past the brush-pushing sweepers, drove up into the Strand, combed the river-leading side streets, knowing he was too bloody late and there was nothing he could do but wait upon events, upon the expected brandishing of Hedge, consoling himself as best he could with the thought that Hedge had had in any case to be left with his captors and things hadn't in fact been made any the worse. It had been a chance that hadn't come off and that was all.

★   ★   ★

Seddon's Way had become a nerve centre: the rest of the night was passed between the telephone and another personal visit to the bowels of the earth, where still no explosive device had been found: all was mystery still. With zero hour now sufficiently positive, the anti-measures were stepped up: from the time the underground stations opened, a full muster of police and troops in plain clothes would be on duty in every station on the network, and along the platforms, mingling with the crowds, observing, noting, ready to apprehend anyone who appeared to be acting in the least suspiciously. Shard, knowing it had to be done, groaned inwardly: if things went wrong, and so far there was no indication that they would go right, a lot of police and soldiers from out of town were going to die with London's commuters by sunset.

★   ★   ★

And those telephone calls:

Head of Security to Shard: 'All stops out now, Chief Superintendent. Is there anything further you want?'

'Yes, sir. I ask again, closure of the system.'

'I'm in agreement with that and I've pressed it. I'm awaiting something positive from Downing Street. I've put the point that there's no further need for secrecy, seeing our friends have shown their hand. I'll be in touch again.'

'Keep pressing, sir,' Shard said. 'By the way, I'd like a word of advice. How far do we go in protecting Hedge?'

'What d'you mean by that?'

'I mean, the opposition could be bluffing to some extent. Hedge may be their card, not the underground. If that emerges, sir, who's more vital—Hedge, or the two men arriving at Heathrow?'

There was a pause. 'Do *you* think they're bluffing, Shard?'

'No, sir. It was just a point I felt should be made.'

'It's noted. But that won't be your decision. Your job's to stop *anything* happening.' The line went off: Shard sat back, thinking: thank you very much! Then the security line went again, this time the Home Office, who had Partington of London Transport with them, to check the last-minute police dispositions and to give telephone time to the top doctor and his fears of disease. After that, the Yard and Hesseltine, in conference with the military command. His head buzzing, Shard snatched a moment at eight in the morning to carry out his promise to Hedge by ringing his wife in Eaton Square: that was easier than he'd feared. Hedge's wife was used to Hedge's comings and goings and didn't ask questions.

Then Beth, which was far from good. Though she, too, understood the impossibilities of police life, the times when a husband couldn't drop everything and phone home, her voice held a hint of rebellion. She had decided to stay put in Ealing even if he couldn't keep on popping home: and today she was going shopping. With her mother.

'Where, for God's sake?'

'Don't shout, and don't sound so stupid, Simon. The West End, where else?'

He lost control: he was dead tired, dead worried, and he couldn't, when not dealing with authority, hold it in any more. 'Don't you dare!' he said in a cracking voice, more violently than he would ever have spoken to an erring DC. 'Don't you bloody dare!'

Like once before, she hung up on him; he called back and she didn't answer. He sat trembling, sweating, arms stiff against his desk. Beth's West End shopping days followed a fairly rigid pattern: arrive High Street

220

Kensington half past ten, give or take five minutes, coffee at Barker's, round the shops in the High Street, then farther east and lunch at one o'clock at Swan and Edgar's. In the afternoon, Regent Street and Piccadilly and back to Swan and Edgar's for a late tea. After that, home to Ealing via—when her mother was with her—Clapham Common to see an aunt. Always on these occasions she left Swan and Edgar's at five o'clock, down to the Piccadilly Line, change at Charing Cross for Waterloo and Clapham on the Northern ... today, right slap into trouble at near enough zero hour.

Shard closed his eyes, trying to shut out imagination.

CHAPTER SIXTEEN

Outwardly, London was normal that early morning: the tube trains, with their loads predominantly of manual workers and shift workers, carried also other men: men whose faces were more than usually watchful, but not so as to show too openly that they were not bound on mundane matters. In the booking halls and along the platforms more plain-clothes men lingered, but again not too ostentatiously, spending a while on the subterranean platforms and then ascending the escalators as the men from above, alternating their watch duties, descended into the depths. These men had come anonymously from the various police districts and from London's military barracks, leaving in ones and twos to merge with the commuters at the widespread stations of the underground network. London was no more depressed, no more anxious than ever it was: the gloom on the faces of the swaying passengers, sitting, and as morning wore on into rush hour, standing, waiting for the week's end so that they could begin to live, was due to no more than the normal baffled hopelessness of life in continuing shortages and financial crisis. The newspapers carried headlines of threatened strikes and more inflation, of power difficulties, of worsening balances of payments and reduced exports and of outrages in foreign parts: nothing of any top-brass terrorist get-together in Venezuela or of any physical happening about to break here in London.

★   ★   ★

After breakfasting early, the Prime Minister had called a meeting of his Cabinet: this meeting took place in Downing Street, with outsiders called in to advise authority. Hedge's boss was present, to press the Prime Minister for total closure underground—to press again, after receipt of a negative in the early hours of the morning. The Prime Minister, a porcine figure at the centre of affairs, was pale but composed: composed enough to manifest a customary obstinacy.

'I can't possibly concede that,' he said, tight-lipped, heavy jowls overhanging his shirt-collar. 'Surely you must see that?'

'I'm afraid I don't, sir. I've already said, there's no point whatsoever in maintaining all this secrecy.'

'On the contrary!' the Prime Minister snapped.

'Then may I ask why?'

'Certainly. I refuse to admit defeat, that's briefly why.' Small eyes stared round the polished mahogany. 'We are not going to let these wicked men get away with their demands, we are not going to surrender to blackmail. These men must be apprehended and punished, made an example of. Any other course would be totally disastrous!' There was a degree of rhetoric now, as though the television cameras loomed. 'The people of this country are looking to us to settle this sort of effrontery once and for all. Only by doing that can we maintain our authority, only by doing that can we all sleep easily in our beds at night, and go about our normal business in the daytime.' The Prime Minister leaned forward, staring directly at the Head of Security and emphasising his words with a fist that thumped the table before him.

'Closure would be fatal. Our plain-clothes men would not only lose their cloak, but we would be handing the whole underground network to these people on a plate. With no trains running through the tunnels, they could do precisely as they liked—and without a doubt the threat would materialise.'

'But without enormous casualties, sir.'

'Agreed—certainly. But in my view it's a risk we have to take.' The Prime Minister waved his hand. 'That is all I have to say on the point, except this, and it's vitally important: we must not start a panic before the event—or before what must be circumvented, rather—because to do that would be to invite very great public pressure on us to release the two incoming air passengers for their onward flight to Maracaibo—in other words, to give in. Which, gentlemen, is, I repeat, something I refuse absolutely to do.'

★   ★   ★

'Flat refusal,' the chief reported to Shard.

Shard's stomach twisted. 'Has he no feeling at all, sir?'

'We must see all points of view, Shard. I've turned somersaults, looking at the thing from every angle I can. Result, I have to admit a certain logic. It's cruel, it's devilish, but in the end it could turn out the best way.'

'If we can cut them out—yes!'

'That's our job, isn't it? We mustn't fail, that's all.' Direct eyes looked into Shard's. 'How's it going?'

'Let's say ... as well as can be expected! All dispositions made—every man has photostats of the identikit pictures—'

'What for? When these people approach the crunch, they're not going to use anyone who's identifiable, are they?'

Shard gave a somewhat rueful smile. 'Point taken, sir. We were aware of that, but everything had to be covered. So far as humanly possible, it has been. I think—I hope—I can guarantee our friends aren't going to infiltrate the system unseen.'

'That's a big guarantee, Shard. The rush hour figures run into millions.'

'I did qualify it, sir.'

'Yes. You're not, in fact, all that hopeful—are you?'

'No, sir. I've been relying—maybe too much—on getting a line on them again before they went underground. Even now ... I doubt if they'll all be going underground. I won't be sleeping in this, sir.'

The chief gave a harsh laugh. 'I didn't think you would! What are your movements going to be?'

'I have one more line to follow up, sir. If that fails, then I'm going underground.'

'Whereabouts? A roving commission, all over?'

'Perhaps. But I'm concentrating on that hunch of mine: the under-river sections. From somewhere around four p.m. that's where I'll be—under the Thames, with Partington.'

The chief nodded. 'I wish you luck, Shard, and I admire your guts.' He paused. 'This line—can you tell me?'

'It's a shot in the dark, that's all.'

'Aimed which way?'

Shard said, 'Towards Hedge. I disobeyed orders—I tailed him. I can guarantee I wasn't seen, but I've a nasty feeling I left a stone unturned. I'm going to turn it if I can.'

★　★　★

It had hit him, shortly after he had telephoned Beth: hit him like a sledge-hammer blow. Hedge, the almost deserted Embankment—*almost deserted*. What in fact had there been? The cruising police patrol car, a river-gazing dropout, the lovers, and the two street-sweepers, nocturnally propelling their mobile dustbin. Why he hadn't ticked over ... that so-sudden disappearance of Hedge in virtually no time at all, and that perambulating garbage bin on wheels, big enough perhaps to take a man? Shard grinned without humour, with a cold hand gripping his heart: Hedge, shoved in with the street sweepings, bedded down beneath flung-in layers of old cigarette packets, gritty dust and used contraceptives. Hedge was heavy, but he wasn't tall, he could be pushed down to fit. There were such things as hypodermics to keep a man quiet while he was trundled off to obscurity. It was a possibility: but why not a car, for God's sake? To interview the two road sweepers might be a sheer waste of time: in all probability, if the theory was right, they wouldn't be on the payroll in any case, they would just have been dressed up and planted. It probably wasn't all that hard to nick a hand-cart: that, in itself, could be the starting point. As to why not a car: well—you didn't normally think, if you were putting a chase in hand, of opening up all London's garbage carts. Shard hadn't, for one.

Neat! And worth a little time.

From Seddon's Way Shard rang the Greater London Council, was put in touch with the refuse disposal people. They had had no report of any apparatus missing from Westminster. Yes, they would check, if it was urgent, with other areas.

'It's urgent,' Shard said. 'Very, very urgent.'

All right, they said, they would ring back. Just over an hour later, at ten thirty-five, they did so: a garbage collection cart had been reported missing believed stolen from a depot south of the river. It had since turned up again, abandoned in a side turning off Ludgate Hill, and there had been traces of blood on the contents. Shard noted the address of the depot to which the hand-cart had been taken, said his thanks, and rang off. So far, so good—but so what? It looked like it could be the vehicle of vanishment, but it was unlikely it would yield up any leads to its pushers. Fingerprints ... no value there! Shard didn't want identities at this stage, he wanted bodies. He sat irresolute, baffled, sweating: having taken time on this, it could be worth finishing before he linked up with Partington of London Transport for the final throw. He left his office and walked quickly through to Leicester Square underground station, crowded with men and women going about their ordinary occasions, like Beth ... he shivered. Better not to think about that hung-up call, the subsequently unanswered line. To go out on a note of bitter quarrel ... he shut his mind firmly, kept his eyes on the watch. He identified the other watchers, the police and troops, without much difficulty: to the initiated they couldn't fail to look the part, however weird the clothing and the hair styles. One bearded layabout with bead hangings and an old lady's cast-off fur coat he recognised as a Detective Sergeant from the Yard's heavy squad: they had worked together in the past and the recognition was mutual. And only fleeting: an outsider would have noticed nothing between them. The anti-measures were in gear but they wouldn't, couldn't be enough despite brave words to the chief. Shard felt icy cold in the tube's fug as he rattled away towards the garbage depot, passing beneath the Thames to Waterloo and beyond. The train's hollow booming sound rang in his ears like a death knell. At Kennington, quite by chance, he saw Partington on the platform, and caught his attention. Partington joined him, and they stood together, backs to the rear-end bodywork of the coach, staring down the gangway—stood and, in low voices, talked. Partington was on a general check along all sections, just keeping an eye on things. Hope was at a low ebb but everything, Partington said, was ready to cope if it did happen.

'Gas, water and electricity. Sewers. Medical services. They expect epidemics to start within days.'

'Weil's Disease?' Shard asked sardonically.

'And other things, also largely rat-borne or from water pollution.' Partington looked sick already. 'How d'you rate the chances?'

'We just keep our fingers crossed,' Shard answered. Partington didn't make any response. When Shard got out he left the train as well and walked along the platform, conferring with a man wearing heavy rubber waders like a fisherman, as Shard went up and out to the fresh air. At the garbage depot Shard was shown the hand-cart. he emptied it out, going minutely through the contents like a beachcomber, observing the blood that could be Hedge's. A load of London filth, which he examined with growing despondency and hopelessness. A waste of time: an old shoe, lashings of grit and mud, the inevitable empty Durex packet ex-Victoria Embankment gardens, some broken glass that could have accounted for the blood, a discarded paperback, illustrated, entitled *Breasts and Bottoms*, bus and tube tickets, a glove . . . all the usual, no doubt, but not perhaps as much as would normally be garnered, in the interest of accommodating Hedge. Despite despondency and the pressures of the time element, Shard did his beachcombing with diligent thoroughness. The break-through, or what could be the break-through, came on the inside of a torn-open cigarette packet: what looked at first sight like the meanderings of a spider drowning in blood resolved into a shakily written address. Shard felt a surge of excitement: good for Hedge! Hedge, who could have overheard some talk, had used his blood with useful effect. Presumably in total darkness, Hedge's blood-dipped finger had managed to bring some light into the situation. The address, short and simple, was 16 Foxton, whatever that might mean, and clearly it had to mean something: people shut in mobile dustbins a-trundle along the Embankment didn't use their blood and energy just to while away the journey. Shard rose from his knees and demanded, and got pronto, a street guide: Foxton Road, Foxton Court, Foxton Lane and Foxton Buildings were all in the vicinity of Notting Hill, W2. Shard lost no time: back below the river, he went straight to New Scotland Yard and a word with the Assistant Commissioner Crime.

'Wild goose chase,' was Hesseltine's opinion, 'and heavy on manpower just now. I'm spread to the limit, Simon.'

Shard pressed. 'I agree they may have flown. But Hedge has given us something and we can't let it go. It can't do any harm, even taking the worst view, can it?'

'No,' Hesseltine said, sounding dubious. Then he nodded. 'All right, Simon, we'll have to go in and check, I suppose, but it's going to mean draining away all my reserves, and I mean all. Do it quickly and let me have my men back.'

'Will do,' Shard said. 'Now for the details.'

*　　　*　　　*

Each possible address had to be gone over simultaneously: it was, Shard said, the only way. To attack one, with only a one-in-four chance of choosing right, would simply risk alerting the others—the area was not large. It

231

would be a biggish operation in the context of the depleted manpower availability: Shard wanted four cars, with four men each plus driver, to cover the four addresses, and he wanted the men armed. To this, Hesseltine made no objection: to arm police was serious, but was clearly demanded by the situation. They would be issued with Model 10 Smith and Wessons fitted with the four-inch 'heavy' barrel. Each of the cars would carry a specially trained marksman equipped to kill efficiently. Shard, feeling the heady breath of a last-minute success despite the chances of the birds having flown—a real enough possibility—asked for, and got, a command car for his own use. He would, he said, remain on the perimeter and be available the moment his radio called him to whichever address proved to be the right one.

Within twenty minutes of Shard's arrival at the Yard, the cavalcade was on its way in plain cars and the beat men around the Foxton area of W2 had been warned on their personal radios to keep a distant surveillance on the four given addresses.

CHAPTER SEVENTEEN

Rain had set in: even the weather was against them. The underground system would be carrying more people than on a fine, dry day. The police motorcade swished along wet streets, hemmed into the jams: Shard was consumed with impatience now. The lead was good—was first-class if it wasn't too late. And every second counted: Shard seethed with impotence, hating the guts of joyriders who blocked progress, hindered vital things. He kept, as he drove, an automatic-reflex lookout, the more careful as he neared the area of all the Foxtons. He saw nothing of interest, no familiar faces, not that he had actually expected to. On the fringe of Foxtonia, just around the corner from Foxton Road in fact, Shard stopped and waited. Because there was nowhere else to wait, he waited on a yellow line: just a single one, but a beat man came across after a while to remind him of the twenty-minute loading limit. A helmet descended to window level and Shard told the policeman who he was, adding a warning: 'Don't react, laddie. You know the form?'

'Yes, sir.'

'Anything happening—you know where?'

'Not a thing, sir, except the patrol cars'll be going in now.'

'Yes. No sight of the birds?'

'No, sir.'

'How about the nick?'

Puzzlement: 'The nick, sir?'

'A busy day for customers?'

233

'Oh—I get you, sir! Yes, you could call it busy. I didn't know there were so many Arabs in the whole country, sir.'

Shard grinned, nodded a dismissal. 'Make yourself scarce. I'll not be here long—I hope!' The constable straightened and went on with his beat. Shard spared a thought for the nick, all the London nicks and their long-suffering station officers. Identikits were not always easy to identify from: there would be any God's amount of suspects wheeling in for a check-out. If it were not so bloody serious, Shard thought, it would have its funny side: all that gesticulation, all the offended innocence! The trouble was, it took time, it soaked up watching manpower, and it gummed the works, but it was all inevitable. He drummed his fingers on the steering-wheel, watched the crowds: like so much of London, all colours. Time pressed hard on Shard: zero hour was now just a matter of five to six hours off. Thoughts of the time-scale loosened his guts, increased his blood pressure, brought him out in a sweat, made sitting tamely behind the wheel into a supreme effort of will. Again he thought of Beth: fought the images down, layering them with others: he was selfish to think about his own problems. All London faced similar ones, even if they didn't yet know—and the cops, of course, did know and were mostly in his boat with him. That young constable he'd just spoken to: there was

234

probably a wife, maybe children, pretty certainly a mother and father. It didn't do to think: coppers shouldn't think other than constructively. Shard went on drumming, still feeling the wateriness inside. Probably coppers should never even get married ...

His radio stirred: his call-sign. He flicked a switch 'S 2, over.'

'Jigger 4. Contact, contact. Over.'

'Right, I'm coming in. Out.' Shard snapped off the switch. Jigger 4 had taken Foxton Lane. Shard let in his gears, took the corner fast, going quickly up through the gearbox. Along Foxton Road, another corner around Foxton Buildings and into Foxton Lane. Outside Number 16, the police car, empty and unattended. Something settled in Shard's gut: a knot of apprehension though he didn't know quite why. He slammed on his brakes just ahead of Jigger 4 and got out fast, up the dirty stone steps with his gun in his hand, and into the hall. The hall was long and narrow and dirty, with peeling wallpaper and paint old and cracked into spider's-web patterns. And there was silence ... Shard went along the hall towards a door at the end, glancing up a staircase as he went. He was by the door when the daylight went and he heard a slam: he whirled round fast, flattening his body to the wall. From inside the front door there was a vivid flash and lead zinged past the end of his nose. He fired back blind, aiming for where he fancied the flash had been. He heard movement. A laugh came back to him from close by, and he went into a crouch, firing again. Something came down on his head, hard, and all his world was filled with flashes of red, green, orange, blue, a kaleidoscope that ended in funereal black.

★   ★   ★

He felt sick: he heard himself groaning, retching, but didn't at first connect the sounds with himself. They seemed disembodied and somehow unreal despite the rising sickness that culminated, within moments of his returning consciousness, in a gush of vomit.

'Dirty beast.'

The voice was a woman's. Shard, his head reeling and spinning, opened his eyes but saw only more flashes, whorls of light that gave him pain so that he closed his eyes again. A moment later, just as he was realising that he was wet through already, a dash of cold water took him over the head. He gasped and shivered. His senses were coming back: he was brought to full awareness by a familiar scent. To a point, the hunt had been successful, Hedge's diligent and brave lead a good one: he had made a find all right, though not in the manner intended.

Opening his eyes again, he saw the guns

236

staring him in the face from all round: one, two, three, four, five, two of them in the hands of Terry and Nigel from Stalling Busk, Terry's eyes as fishlike, as coldly pink-rimmed as ever. Nadia Nazarrazeen, not underground at all, was well supported. His lips felt stiff and liable to crack, and his tongue was as dry as a bone in spite of the water-dousing; but he managed a question: 'What happened?'

The woman—and even in his sickness and his gall she was attractive—laughed in his face. 'You were neatly tricked, Simon Shard, that is what happened!'

'The radio call?'

'Yes.'

'One of your mob? But the voice—'

'Was a policeman's. Don't cast blame—he had no option. There were guns ... one went off after he had called you.'

'You killed him?'

She nodded. 'All are dead. Open your eyes properly, and look.'

Feeling cold as death himself, Shard lifted his head, looked where the girl was pointing. Across the carpet, on a long cushioned sofa against the farther wall, four men sat, with a fifth, Jigger 4's driver, on the floor with his back to the wall. Five plain-clothes men, very still, eyes open and vacantly staring, all with their front clothing charred by guns fired close, and blood still redly drooling from small holes.

Shard felt choked, unable to breathe. 'You bitch,' he said. 'You filthy, murderous little bitch.'

She didn't mind that: she went on smiling and there was no retaliation. Just the steady guns to inhibit movement. Shard's head was bursting. He said, 'You've put yourself in a spot, haven't you?'

'How so?'

'My bosses—'

'No, no. They are satisfied, and will remain satisfied for long enough. A report was sent by radio, that you had found nothing precise but were following a possible lead to Knockholt Pound.' Again she laughed.

'Why Knockholt Pound?'

'It is a funny name, and tickled my sense of humour. You may wish to ask about the cars, yours and your men's: I shall tell you, Simon Shard, they have been driven away and left.'

'But someone will come—'

'Yes, in time. But we shall not be here.'

'Where, then?'

'You will see. You will come with us.' She shrugged: Shard became aware of her breasts, full dark cream in the low-cut dress, the cleft clearly exposed. 'We didn't want you, we have no need of you, but you came into the district and now we cannot leave you. It is on your own head.' She lifted her wrist, looked at a tiny watch, richly jewelled and golden. 'Try now to get up, Simon Shard.'

Delay was the obvious answer: too obvious. He tried it and was discouraged with a man's boot against his side, kicking painfully. Then he was dragged upright and set on his feet, the guns nudging. Sickness returned; retching, bringing up his very stomach lining, he was manhandled to the door. His head throbbed: it felt as if it had grown to the proportions of a mountain range, with a very special peak dead top central.

★   ★   ★

The dead policemen were left behind, sitting upright in their silence: it didn't matter any more, Nadia Nazarrazeen said with total indifference. Shard enquired, as they went out into a back garden, small and derelict, about her future safety *vis-à-vis* the law. Whatever might happen in regard to the main threat, she was already many times a killer. Was she going to enjoy a life sentence for, as it were, *en route* murder?

'That is taken care of,' was all she would say. Part of the bargain to be made? They all crossed the garden towards a wrought-iron gate into a back alley—Shard and Nazarrazeen, Terry and Nigel, and three dark-skinned Arabs in Western jeans, Levis. Terry looked out, then nodded. He and Nigel went off to the right along the alley, vanishing round a bend. The rest of the party headed left at a brisk pace that made Shard's head worse. At the end of the alley was a car, a Volvo. One of the Arabs unlocked the driver's door and got in, opening the other doors. Nadia Nazarrazeen got into the front passenger seat, the other three squeezed in the back, surrounding Shard: a tight fit, and uncomfortable. The car drove off fast, no more delays. It made into the heart of London, right up into the West End—right along Victoria Street, past New Scotland Yard. Shard's chief emotion now was amazement at effrontery, at total confidence. A whole car-load of Middle Eastern faces on a day like this, and his own face known personally to quite a few London coppers, sergeants and above anyway ... if this wasn't a risk he didn't know what was! But in the event no one looked at them twice: there were other things on lay minds, this not yet being one of them; and the police mind was largely underground. In safety, in anonymity, the Volvo purred across Westminster Bridge, over the Thames, lying now not below rain but below a clear blue sky with the cloud distant over north London. Buses ran past, taxis, cars ... below on the water tugs chuffed ahead of their strings of laden or ballasted barges, up and down the river. From Westminster Pier a river-bus set off gaily, leaving the landing-stage and swinging round to head for Tower Bridge, and HMS *Belfast*, and the *Cutty Sark*, and the Royal Naval College at Greenwich, with men, women and children bulging the decks and dangling dangerously over the guardrails. If they didn't come back too soon, they would be safe, maybe ... the Volvo slowed, stopped briefly on the bridge, and the girl got out, flipping her hand in a goodbye gesture and walking towards a flight of stone steps to the river-walk below, not hurrying. More effrontery: Shard had to admire her for her supreme self-confidence. The Volvo was driven on, turned around a one-way system by St Thomas's Hospital, and back once again over Westminster Bridge: no sign now of Miss Nazarrazeen. On the north bank the Volvo turned right, going along the Embankment where Shard had mounted his abortive tail in the early hours. Beyond Blackfriars Bridge it entered a maze of smelly side alleys between New Bridge Street and St Paul's, coming eventually to rest behind a dry-cleaners' van stopped with its rear doors close to a manhole in the centre of the alley. The Volvo was driven equally close, so that its front bumper was almost at the lip of the manhole. As the Volvo stopped, the rear doors of the van were opened up: a big man dressed as a sewerman leaned down and banged on the manhole cover with a thinnish iron bar, sending some kind of signal: two, three, two. Then stop. Looking up, he

241

grinned through the Volvo's windscreen at the driver. Then he jumped down and levered out the manhole cover. The moment the cover was manipulated out of its socket, Shard was hustled from the car and taken to the lip of the exposed sewer entry: looking down with his head swimming, he saw the metal rungs of a vertical ladder leading into blackness. One of the men from the car swung himself down first: then Shard. As he began to lower himself into the gloom and the rising stench, Shard heard both the van and the Volvo start up: they would be away as soon as the whole party was down, as soon as the manhole cover had been slotted back in position ... he looked up, saw the last pair of legs swing down above his head, then the blackout of the last circle of daylight. From below, and distantly, came a low sound, a mixture of sounds—what seemed vaguely like moving water, plus a hum of electric motors, plus disjointed booming sounds. The smell increased and the darkness thick and tangible, remained as they went down rung by rung. Then, suddenly, the darkness went: far below them still, a bright light came on, throwing strange shadows as it rose past the man climbing down below Shard. The metal ladder shaking under their weight against the brickwork, they continued down to a platform above a moving river of water, where two more men were waiting: more sewermen, men in thigh-high waders, flushers maybe, the troglodytes who cleaned the channels under their gangers. They carried safety-lamps that would glow red if they encountered air contamination, and they carried guns.

One of them asked, 'Who's this?' He indicated Shard.

'A detective who grew too curious.'

'Dangerous—isn't it?'

'His visit is well authenticated,' the dark-skinned man said, 'You have no need to worry. Is everything ready at control?'

The flusher nodded, drawing the back of a hand across his nostrils. 'All ready.'

'The explosives?'

'They're down.' In the electric light, Shard recognised the look of fear in the man's eyes. 'Listen, when do we clear out, eh?'

'There'll be time for that. For the present, you're all right here.' The dark man's tone was hard. 'And here you stay, remember that! You are in this very deep, my friend, deeper by far than you now are in the sewer!' He laughed, but there was no humour.

'Oh, I'll stay,' the sewerman said. 'Just give us good warning for out—that's all I ask. Right out of bloody London!'

'Yes, this you shall have.' The man looked towards Shard and his companions of the descent. 'Come now, there is some way yet to go.'

243

'Mr Shard doesn't answer, sir,' the switchboard reported to Assistant Commissioner Hesseltine.

'From where—Seddon's Way?'

'Yes, sir. Shall I try the FO, sir?'

'Yes, do that.' Hesseltine drummed his fingers and waited: hoped Shard was getting places but began to suffer frustration's pangs; tried hard to force an occupation of his mind with other work. He hadn't too long to wait: today the name of Simon Shard, Detective Chief Superintendent, had its built-in call for speed. But again it was blank: no knowledge. Hesseltine was impatient but not yet worried: there had been absolutely no reason to doubt the authenticity of the radio call that had said Shard was chasing a lead. Anxiety might start up later: Hesseltine, as the top cop he was, used a part of his mind to prepare for that anxiety: if and when Shard didn't show, there would be someone else to look out for in the booking halls and subway stations. Very likely he was there already: no lead after all, and so straight down as pre-indicated.

★　　　★　　　★

Shard, feeling ill, waded the horrible scummy water flowing through the sewer, flowing and smelly, filthy collection from the drains and God knew where else. The procession had two torches, powerfully beamed, provided by one of the custodians of the platform below the manhole. They walked in a crouching attitude for what seemed to Shard an immensely long way. At intervals, widely spaced, there were more platforms and sometimes more lights: electricity cables ran right the way along. It was a horrible experience in that close foetid airlessness, and Shard's heart was sinking with his hopes: it was getting too near the end. He could see no way out, short of getting hold of the guns that were guarding him, and that wasn't on: just one move out of turn, that was all they needed ... and the rushing black sewer-water waited to hurry his body away. It was no consolation that all things, good or bad, had to come to an end: and it was no consolation that the present journey ended, some way farther along, in a clamber up onto a kind of walkway that led to a concrete-lined chamber situated off one of the under-manhole platforms, a chamber filled with electrically operated machinery and a plastic-covered, padded bench on which sat, of all people to find in a sewer, Hedge.

Hedge, who was being guarded by four Middle Eastern gunmen, didn't appear to notice that Shard was off colour. He was looking thoroughly wretched, but he improved quickly

245

when he saw Shard. 'It's you!' he said unnecessarily; then looked mortified, as though he shouldn't have said a word.

'It's all right,' Shard said. 'They know who I am.' He added a sir, since Hedge was supposed to be the boss man, little though he looked the part at the moment. 'Hand-cart—I presume?'

'Yes. Cigarette packet?'

Shard nodded. 'I think that was a mistake—sir. If I may say so.' In the electric light, he studied his fingernails for a moment, watched by the four gunmen, who were now in process of taking over Shard himself from his escort. The hand-over made, the escort left, going back the way they had come. Shard went on, 'It only led to more deaths—five policemen.'

'Oh, my God. It seemed a good idea.'

'Yes. Maybe it was me—my personal bungle. I've a nasty feeling it was, in fact.' Shard stared at the Arab faces. He said, 'I'm beginning to get the drift. On the way in, your friends weren't talking ... but I didn't really need to ask. This sewer runs close enough to a section of tube tunnel for you to cut through—right?'

One of the gunmen smiled. 'This is correct.'

'Clever—to have got away with it! The sewers were one of the items on our list. But this you'll know, of course—'

'Yes, we know. We found it easy—'

246

'Traitors, quick-money bastards, in your pay?'

'That, yes. Also stories from the German POW camps. It was easy to hide the entrance, easy to carry away all we dug out.'

'Where is this entrance?'

'Here,' the Arab said. 'Here, in this compartment. Your Mr Hedge is sitting over it at this moment. I will show you—it is time we began to make ready, in any case.' He took a screwdriver from a pocket and began removing the heavy screws holding down the legs of the bench, screws that passed right through eyelet-holes in a rough floor covering of heavy-duty canvas and on into metal sockets set in the concrete beneath. He put each screw carefully into his pocket: a reflex action, result of constant repetition, like the wartime escapees? Shard watched: when the operation was complete, the Arab glanced up at Hedge, still sitting in state on the bench.

'If you please,' he said with oily politeness.

Hedge stared, then ticked over. He rose huffily, clutching at Shard for support as the gunman pulled the vacated bench away from the wall and drew back the canvas floor-covering. From outside came a hair-raising scurrying sound, followed by an outbreak of squeaking. Hedge looked ill.

'Rats,' Shard said briefly. 'Fighting.'

'I know! They're not the first, Shard, not the

first by a long chalk. I feel pretty bad as a matter of fact, and I blame those damn rats!'

'It's much too soon for Weil's Disease to show. Or to be caught,' he added with hasty reassurance, noting the extra look on Hedge's face. Then he turned his attention to the bared floor: there was a neatly cut square of concrete being lifted out, to leave an entry fully adequate to take a man of Hedge's bodily thickness. Behind this came armful after armful of cottonwool packets, used no doubt as a sound damper: when it was all out, and there was a hell of a lot of it, together with a square of wood cut to hold it in place below, Shard heard the hollow rattle of a tube train tearing along the tunnel somewhere underneath.

Shard swallowed, asked, 'Where exactly are we? Which section?' He already knew the answer, ninety-nine percent sure and certain: from the Arab confirmation came, the final check that he'd been right from more or less the start. The cut channel led through the floor of the sewer's power house, through the heavy London clay, into the underground system, with just a matter of less than a foot yet to be excavated before the final cut was made into the Northern Line a little way before it reached out below the London river.

CHAPTER EIGHTEEN

Shard sat on the bench, more than a little thankfully. He met the eye of Hedge. 'This, you knew?'

Hedge nodded greenly. 'They told me. I've been here since I was brought down.'

Shard opened his mouth to say something irritable in response to a stupid statement, but decided not to: it would have been too cruel. Hedge was right out of his element: you couldn't compare, unless you wanted to be very rude, the Foreign Office atmosphere with that of a sewer. Hedge may have been the front screen, but basically he was the backroom boy, the lurker in the shadows. There was no room for intrigue down here in the bowels of the earth, an apt phrase considering the aroma; it was a place for facing the facts of life and death. Up there—a comparative phrase—for a while, was life: down in the pit so assiduously dug out lay death for the many within hours. Shard's job remained the same as ever: to stop it taking place. It sounded easy when said fast. His mind was working in top gear but as yet was finding no clear straight motorway of progression: it was on a racing circuit, round and round and back constantly to the starting grid. On that starting grid were set certain factors and certain virtual impossibilities: neither he nor Hedge could contact the surface, make any report that would tell the waiting world that this threat was utterly for real, that if the gentlemen coming into Heathrow from the Lebanon were not on-sent to Maracaibo, London had more or less had it. On the constructive side, the side of his duty to prevent blast-off, Shard could see no chink of light at all...

He asked, 'That hole. Does it stay open now?'

'Yes. From some time ago—since you came down, Mr Shard—not one person will come through the street entry and live to go back again.' The spokesman dusted his hands together. 'We are ready—ready now, all the angles covered.'

'The explosive?'

'Yes, that is ready, and will be lowered into the tunnel shortly now—'

'And your leading lady?'

The man smiled, the teeth a white flash across the dark face. 'An apt title. She is ready too—'

'She's down here, down in the sewers?'

'No. She remains on the surface.'

'Until when?'

Another smile: 'Until for ever, Mr Shard. From the surface she is in control. From the surface she will speak to your authorities by radio. She will be in contact with us also, when she wishes. Down here there is a telephone . . . and we have other persons working for us—'

'People in the sewage control?'

'Yes. And elsewhere.'

There was a brief silence, broken by Hedge. 'None of us are going to get out, Shard. I suppose you've guessed that, haven't you?'

Shard grinned. 'Never say die.' Hedge looked terrible: Shard wondered when he would crack, when he would blurt out the truth: that he was not the summit, however close. To do that wouldn't help him, wouldn't save his life, but the urge to try his luck might become overwhelming. Shard went on, doing his best to inject a decent confidence into Hedge, 'They won't gain anything by leaving us here, you know—leaving us to die like rats.' He caught the eye of the Arab who had been doing the talking. 'Will you?'

The Arab shrugged. 'I cannot say yet. This depends.'

'On what?'

'Why, on the reaction of your people when the aircraft from the Lebanon comes in. If there is no co-operation . . . why, then I think you will die, yes.'

'And you, and these others?' Shard waved a hand: the faces were watchful, tense—fanatical. Confirmation was totally unnecessary: there was something almost Japanese . . . Shard remembered the wartime *kamikaze* pilots, those

251

suicide lovers who had hurled their explosives-packed planes onto the decks of the allied aircraft-carriers, battleships, cruisers ... like them, these Arabs would die for the cause if that should become necessary. You couldn't win against that sort of mental attitude. Shard asked, gesturing towards Hedge, 'Why were you so anxious to have my chief here?'

'You have not guessed?'

'Well—perhaps. The safe-conduct for your airborne friends?'

'All the way to Maracaibo,' the Arab said, nodding. 'Extra insurance, a valuable life in jeopardy, in case your authorities should close the underground and reduce the threat by eliminating direct casualties on the big scale. They will not want to lose Mr Hedge. Assuming agreement is reached between Miss Nazarrazeen and your Foreign Office, and your Prime Minister—'

'And the Americans.'

'Yes, and the Americans. Assuming this, your chief, and now you also, will be held here in this place until Miss Nazarrazeen has the information she wants: that the two passengers have landed safely at Maracaibo and have been met by certain persons there. When all this has happened, then there will be freedom. If it does not happen...' The man's expression, his calm matter-of-factness, were meaningful and easily understood. Shard studied Hedge without appearing to do so: he was seeing death staring him in the face, poor Hedge was; a salutary experience. Hedge had never been a field man: he was pure diplomat in basis, having come up via Winchester and Oxford. It was probably Winchester and Oxford that were sustaining him now: Shard hoped devoutly that they would go on doing so. If those admirable institutions should fail Hedge, Shard was never going to be forgiven for being witness to the result.

★   ★   ★

Lead weighted, the hands of Shard's watch approached five p.m. The atmosphere was terrible—both in a mental sense and a physical one: the stench they had almost got used to, but the miasma was still vile enough to worsen Shard's headache so that he felt almost incapable of constructive thought. Hedge was in a bad way, had kept looking appealingly at Shard as though he urgently wanted conversation, but in fact had not uttered. Shard had an idea that one of the things Hedge would have liked to discuss was the actual likelihood of being released even if the Government gave in to outrageous demands, even if the incoming terrorists should reach Maracaibo in safety. If so, Shard could appreciate his anxiety: Hedge, in the hands of villains, would probably be seen as nice cover for their personal getaway afterwards. If he was, then he would just go on being a hostage right into the foreseeable future, a grim prospect indeed. And always, minute by minute, the fear that in the end they would kill him regardless. Which was not unlikely. During the waiting period the final touches had been put to the preparations: two of the gunmen had gone outside and after a longish absence had come back in carrying a large and obviously very heavy container, suit-case shaped, of black plastic; they had then gone out again and staggered back with another similar container. Both these containers—things from the sewer-water itself, things hidden until now—were covered with slime and wet and brought fresh waves of foetid stink that made Hedge produce his handkerchief speedily. Each container was roped, with a dangling end. One of the gunmen wiped the cases clean.

Shard asked, 'The explosive?'

'Yes. Plutonium bombs . . . a total explosive weight of seven kilogrammes of refined plutonium.'

It was too big, too vast for sane appreciation of the likely effect: the size might sound small enough to the lay person but Shard knew that when the two sections of less-than-critical mass were slammed together by the detonator in each bomb so that the whole became explosive-critical, there would be a holocaust in London.

He felt light-headed. He asked, chiefly for the sake of saying something, anything to keep his sanity, 'How about the radiation—in the meantime? Aren't you worried about all the handling?'

'The containers are, of course, properly lined. No, we are not worried.' Silly question! Shard remembered the lead and biological concrete that retained 99.9 percent of the gamma rays. The Arab went on with his work, calm, unhurried: his whole bearing said success. Shard could hear the trains passing down in the tunnel. The normal out-of-rush-hour intervals varied from four to five minutes, depending on the particular line: Shard racked his brains to remember the interval on the Northern Line. His headache was inhibiting him, but probably it made no difference now. As five p.m. approached he made a time check with his watch: the intervals had narrowed for the rush hour and he made it three minutes. Three minutes, maybe a little less, between trains one of which could have Beth aboard any time now. He felt a shake right through his body: there was nothing he could do, just bloody nothing ... there was always a gun pointed—one at least at any given moment. Shard was drenched in sweat, the sweat of a physical sickness and of terrible dread. Maybe a simple attack: he could be fairly sure of getting one of the bastards before he was mown down,

255

but what good would that do? It wasn't on, in a sense it was the coward's way: he could be—might be—more use yet to Beth alive than dead. And it didn't look as though he would get much physical backing from Hedge if he started any trouble.

At a minute past five one of the men entered the exposed hole, carrying with him a metal cutter on the end of an electric lead and going in along the downward slope on a tended rope. The sounds of his progress faded: a train rattled through below, and the moment it had passed the sounds of cutting came up to the waiting men. These sounds ceased as another train was heard, were resumed when it had passed, an operation repeated time and again until the man came back up, covered in clay. With the tube tunnel itself now finally exposed, the plastic-covered containers of nuclear explosive were pushed to the edge of the hole and lowered a little way into the shaft, with the ends of the ropes secured to a ring-bolt set in the concrete wall of the compartment.

★　　　★　　　★

Hesseltine had rung the Head of Security, that shadowy, anonymous man now deprived of his Hedge screen. 'Shard, sir. Results, nil.'

'Could have slipped past, going under-ground. I'm not too worried, Hesseltine.' There was a pause. 'I fancy you are?'

'I am. I can't see Shard just . . . slipping past unnoticed. My men are pretty good.'

'So are mine, and we do have our methods. I have to go now, Hesseltine. If you want me, and I don't want to be wanted unless it's vital, I'll be at Heathrow.'

'Right. And—good luck!'

There was a laugh. 'Thank you. As a matter of fact, I'll quite likely be safer out there . . . just by obeying the call of duty. What about you?'

Hesseltine said, 'Oh, I'm staying. That's *my* duty.' He cut the call, glancing at a clock on the wall in front of him: four forty-five. In fifty minutes the British Airways VC 10 from Beirut would touch down: no delays, the incoming checks said, she would arrive spot on. At Heathrow now a big cover operation was under way—ostensibly, since the thing couldn't be entirely hidden, a drugs check was in progress. The whole complex swarmed with police, uniform branch and CID plus Special Branch and a number of men from Hedge's outfit, men who worked for Shard and were feeling angry enough to be super-efficient today after hearing that all contact had been lost. Outside airport, around the perimeter, the army was in strength: Guardsmen, Military Police, explosives experts from the Royal Engineers, communications teams from the Royal Signals, armoured vehicles of the Royal Tank Regiment. Some extremely mobile weapons, field guns and rocket launchers, from the Royal Artillery: it was Catterick and Salisbury Plain and Aldershot moved to London Airport, but Hesseltine, sitting in his office at New Scotland Yard, wondered what the heck they expected the army to do. They could scarcely save the underground system: only word from Downing Street could do that now, and it all came down to a simple yes or no to terrorism, field-guns and infantry notwithstanding.

Again Hesseltine looked at his clock: the Prime Minister hadn't much longer in which to pronounce. Hesseltine's thoughts were interrupted by the buzz of his internal line: word via the Commissioner from Downing Street? No: it was the Yard's control-room. 'All ready, sir.'

'Thanks. I'm coming down now.'

*　　*　　*

'Time we were moving, dear,' Mrs Micklam said. 'It's gone five.'

Beth began to gather her shopping. 'All right, Mummy.' She gave a sigh as she groped on the floor of Swan and Edgar's restaurant for her handbag. 'I do hate the rush hour...'

'You know what your aunt's like,' Mrs Micklam said vaguely, and Beth nodded. Mrs

Micklam's sister Olive had set ideas and liked people to dance to her tune. Her views were simple: people who didn't actually come to tea should arrive between five-thirty and six and there was an end to it. Mrs Micklam—surprisingly, Simon Shard had always thought—obeyed her sister; not knowing the present lethal capabilities of a tense situation, she went down with her daughter in Swan and Edgar's lift, right down to the underground level and out into the booking hall at Piccadilly Circus to buy tickets for Clapham Common. There were men hanging about, unobtrusive-looking men who meant nothing to Mrs Micklam but spoke with a fair degree of eloquence to the wife of a Detective Chief Superintendent: wives, if they were intelligent, and Beth was that, found things tended to rub off and develop in them a kind of sixth sense: she knew, that early evening as she and her mother went down the escalator into the bowels of the London clay, that plain-clothes men were watching out for something unknown: it was a feeling given immediacy by Simon's morning call, which had been on her mind all day. He had been so insistent: passing time had told her there had to be a reason. She'd been too angry to give heed, and pride had intervened. Beth gave a sudden shiver of cold and looked sideways at her mother. Mrs Micklam was short and brisk, disliked interference with her laid plans—she was not unlike her sister in Clapham—and would fuss. Beth, who in any case had nothing definite to offer as a reason why they shouldn't go on with their journey, kept her mouth shut and, looking uneasy, got into the first train for Charing Cross at five thirty-one, after letting the crowds at the edge of the southbound platform clear away first. A few minutes after this they got out at Charing Cross to trudge the stairs and subways towards the Northern Line.

* * *

'It's the Americans,' the Prime Minister said in a shaking voice. 'I've had the White House on the line. The President is—insistent. Apart from the fact he wants the men for trial, he's convinced the conference will never get off the ground without them, but if they're allowed to attend...' His voice trailed away, his eyes stared in beseechment at his ministers: men looked away, doodling on blotting-pads and note-taking stationery. 'My hands are tied. No one's more sorry than I. But of course the President's right. These are wicked men, and we can't give in.'

'The President,' someone said sardonically, 'doesn't live in London, Prime Minister.'

'I'm sorry.' The Prime Minister sat down suddenly, put his head in his hands, all bounce gone, leaving flab naked. There was a silence, a silence broken horribly by the tick of a clock, and then by the sound of Big Ben chiming the half-hour from Westminster. The Home Secretary got to his feet, pushing his chair back with a violent movement. He went to a window and stood looking down into the street: the law on guard at the front door; the usual sightseers in Downing Street, none of them knowing, none of them remotely suspecting drama, none of them realising the close proximity of sudden and appalling destruction, the terror that would come when the very streets erupted into a burst of nuclear energy. His face set, the Home Secretary turned from the window and went across the thick carpet, silently, to the Prime Minister's side. He said, 'You face rebellion, Prime Minister.'

The ashen face looked up. 'The people?'

'The Cabinet. I speak for a majority. This, we shall not have. You must think again.'

'But it may not happen. It's too big. In the end, they won't face it.'

'Bluff?' Harshly, the Home Secretary laughed. 'I don't think so! We've plenty of reason to know what these people are capable of, what they've got away with in the past. It's precisely the same principle—'

'Which is why we must not give in, don't you see?' The Prime Minister looked around at the faces of the men of power: his voice still shook,

261

but there was a firmer note. 'I shall not give in, and I know I shall carry some of you with me. I shall not give in, but I will agree, if you wish, to talk. That, at least, will give us more time—that is, if these people are willing to accept delay. May I remind you, no further word has been received.'

★   ★   ★

In the control-room at New Scotland Yard, Assistant Commissioner Hesseltine, joined now by the Commissioner, watched the closed-circuit television screen giving its colour picture of Heathrow. The cameras moved slowly around the buildings, inside and out, telling their tales on unsuspecting inward and outward passengers as they filled the main hall and the bars and lounges, or went through customs and immigration checks. With many others Hesseltine watched closely, eyes narrowed in concentration, seeking out known faces, faces that might give something away, recognising senior CID officers discreetly but minutely watching. Outside, the cameras showed the airport apron, the waiting tenders and fire appliances and baggage-handlers . . . beyond the perimeter it showed the military concentrations, standing-to now, waiting for action orders. So far as possible the troops and armour had been camouflaged from the air with netting, but

Hesseltine knew the villains would be expecting such obvious precautions: the unknown factor lay only in their possible reaction. A little before five thirty-five the noise came up, the whine of jets—a sound that had been heard every few minutes but, this time, checking with his watch, Hesseltine knew without the confirmation that the British Airways VC 10 from Beirut was coming in to touchdown.

The cameras picked it up, glinting in evening sunlight. Hesseltine swallowed, began a nervous twitch of his eyebrows, caught the eye of the Commissioner. As he did so, telephones rang: two calls. Each was taken by a uniformed Chief Inspector. Hesseltine got to his feet, face expectant.

'Downing Street, sir. The Prime Minister will talk to the terrorists.'

'And if the talking doesn't help?'

'No surrender, sir.'

Hesseltine's eyebrows twitched again: he showed no other reaction as he turned to the second call. 'Well?'

'A woman, sir. No name, but she speaks for Power of Islam.'

Hesseltine reached out a hand, and took the call.

CHAPTER NINETEEN

Hesseltine, when the woman's voice had given him the full picture, did his best to keep her talking, giving his experts time to put on their checks.

'It's not within my province, to—'

'You are one of the Assistant Commissioners of Metropolitan Police,' the voice said: it was clear, young, decidedly attractive.

'I still don't equate with the Prime Minister. This is a Prime Ministerial decision. What's Power of Islam?'

There was a laugh. 'Exactly what it implies, Assistant Commissioner. Now, pass on my message without delay. The two men will remain aboard the aircraft at Heathrow until there is an answer. If they are interfered with, then the explosion will come. That is all for now.'

'How do we contact you?' Hesseltine asked.

'You do not. I shall contact you. I shall use you as my telephone exchange.' Another laugh, a confident sound of approaching victory: then the click in Hesseltine's ear. He lobbed the handset towards the Chief Inspector, who caught it and replaced it. Hesseltine turned to the Commissioner.

'They're ready to go, sir. They're in the system.'

'Underground?'

'Except for the woman, the caller.' Hesseltine's face was grim. 'We failed to stop them. This begins not to look too good.'

The Commissioner didn't comment. He said shortly, 'There was a message, I gather. Better do as the lady said.'

Hesseltine took up a phone and asked for Downing Street. He got a secretary but demanded the brass. The Prime Minister himself came on the line. Hesseltine reported: 'Power of Islam's contacted, sir. A woman. She gives you one hour for an affirmative. By six forty the two men from the VC 10 are to transfer to the TWA for Maracaibo. All security forces to be withdrawn from the vicinity of both aircraft. At the first sign of any counter operation, she'll pass the word down into the tube network.'

'I see.' The Prime Minister was calm, but to Hesseltine it sounded very forced, very brittle. 'This woman . . . do you know where she is at this moment?'

'No, sir. We didn't get a chance . . . and she won't be staying put. When she makes contact again, it'll be from somewhere else.' With half an eye, Hesseltine was watching the TV screen, the view of the aircraft from Beirut. The passengers were disembarking, coming down the steps in an ordinary enough fashion. 'I'll call you as soon as she rings again, sir.'

'Please do. And Hesseltine...'

'Sir?'

'When she does call again, say I'm willing to talk.' The Prime Minister hung up. Hesseltine caught the Commissioner's eye.

'He still talks of talk, sir. I don't believe the lady's in a talking mood. Why should she be? She holds all the cards.' The Commissioner gave no response to that; with Hesseltine, after the withdrawal order had been passed to Heathrow, he watched the camera-work from the airport. No time was being lost in compliance, in being very openly seen to comply. The uniforms withdrew: so, it seemed, did everyone else. The VC 10 was left in isolation, as though it were itself a bomb. There was a strange silence, as much as Heathrow could ever be said to be silent, in the immediate vicinity. Tracking up to the aircraft, the cameras showed two dark faces behind one of the cabin ports.

★   ★   ★

In the subterranean machinery room, one of the Arabs answered a telephone that connected with the main sewage control. He listened, saying nothing. Ringing off he spoke to Shard and Hedge. 'The aircraft has landed. Your security forces are being withdrawn.'

266

Hedge stared: he had been getting more and more glassy-eyed, but now there was a flicker of hope. 'The Government's giving in?'

The gunman laughed. 'Bravely said, Mr Hedge! If all your leaders are like you ... but then, they are not down here like you, are they? No, your government has not yet given in. I think they will do so, however. Your Prime Minister wishes to talk, and talk is always good. Was it not your Mr Churchill who said jaw, jaw is better than war, war?'

No answer from Hedge: he had sunk again, head down on his chest. Shard asked, 'Suppose the talk doesn't lead anywhere?'

'You think it will not?'

'I think it's unlikely. The Prime Minister's an obstinate man.'

'Obstinate to the point of—'

'Of what you intend to do? He may be. You know what governments are. London and Washington—Downing Street and the White House—a lack of comprehension that can creep in, mistakes on purpose.' Shard stared at the man, compellingly. 'Do you see what I'm getting at?'

'I think I do not!'

'Then try harder. Those men are very badly wanted, and for plenty of very urgent reasons. Right now, they're on a plate for the eating. The public here and in America, all over the world in fact—they're sick and tired of gunmen, terrorists, getting away with it—'

'Not tired to the point of personal sacrifice!'

'Perhaps not. But governments are in a rather different position. By using a little unclarity . . . by being not too precise . . . they can gain their objective without incurring the opprobrium of intentional callousness. Something, in short, can go wrong. Now do you see?'

The eyes glittered. 'I see, yes. I do not think this will happen. Why do you put it forward?'

Shard grinned tightly, a mere stretch of lips against teeth. 'Because I think you should start to ponder your own death. I've already pondered mine.' He glanced briefly at Hedge: maybe it was the lighting but Hedge had already the appearance of death, and his face was blotched with fright. 'I don't say I want to die, but I can face a certain inevitability. Can you?'

The Arab nodded. 'So easy,' he said. It was simple and direct, the sincere statement of a soldier in battle, a soldier knowing the odds beyond doubt but having something beyond himself to hold fast to. Nevertheless, there was a new look in the dark eyes, a film of fresh sweat on the skin of the face: Shard had made him think again, face death again. The answer might well remain the same, the steadfastness not much dented, but it was a partial step forward, Shard felt, and he pressed.

'All along, you've been prepared to die—I

accept that. But equally, all along you've not really believed you'd have to. You've believed, and you believe still, that we won't face the crunch. You believe, firmly, that we'll cave in. I'm just asking, suppose we don't?'

No answer.

Shard went on, 'If there's no cave-in, we do all die, don't we? I mean you haven't some brilliant safety device up your sleeve, have you?' He nodded towards the dug-out connexion to the tube tunnel. 'When your nuclear device goes off down there, what stops it reaching back up here?'

'Nothing.'

'And right along the sewer?'

'Nothing stops it.'

'You're a brave bastard, I'll say that,' Shard said after a pause. 'Am I right in supposing you intend to blow the tunnel roof, split the clay below the river ... right through to the water?'

'Yes.'

'I doubt if you'll succeed. The force of the blow-out will travel laterally.'

'To some extent, yes. But in fact it will be held in enough to fracture the tunnel roof and the earth above it. Do you wish me to explain, Mr Shard?'

'Yes. I'm interested.'

'Then this is how it will be: when one train has passed through the river section, and has reached the farther bank, the south bank, the next train is approaching the section at the north bank. If and when we down here receive orders to blow, the cases of plutonium bombs will be lowered at the right moment, lowered a little more—until they're suspended for a depth of one foot into the tube tunnel—'

'And the next train along—'

'The next train that enters the section will hit the explosive and detonate the bombs on impact. They're laid in the cases with the plungers sideways—so.' The Arab demonstrated with his hands. 'The plungers plunge, the detonators detonate, the mass becomes critical, all the little neutrons hitting and multiplying, making heat to several millions of degrees centigrade. There is a tremendous explosion—in effect, carried before the train. The rail to roof height of the tunnel is twelve feet six inches. Each car of the train is twelve feet one inch high from rail level to roof—leaving a gap of five inches above and a little beneath also. The width is nine feet eight inches, leaving one foot five inches free on either side. This will provide at least some tamping—'

'Enough?'

'We don't know. But we are very hopeful!'

'Up in Yorkshire,' Shard said, 'your people spoke of a need for more precise tamping, as I understood—'

'There's been a change. Originally we

270

intended to operate differently, but your tunnel security has been good. We were lucky to find an alternative. I think the tamping will be good, but those who live will be the ones who find this out for certain. If it works, then much of the underground system will be flooded, and very quickly—oh yes, there are protections, water-tight screens, but we have taken this into full account. The screening at this end—the vital end, you realise—will be blown up in the explosion itself. So, you see, the water will flood along the line to the north ... irresistible, swelling, deepening ... submerging subways and escalators, drowning your commuters, a catastrophe that will put London's underground transport and many of her sewers and electric cables and gas mains out of use for many months...'

'The voice went on: Shard stopped listening to boastfulness. It was all precisely as he had dreamed it up for himself and his imagination was as good as the voice of fact. He dwelt for a space on the sheer technics: what the man had said, sounded feasible. Partington's advices came back to Shard: each axle of the motor-unit cars carried a nose-suspended sixty horse-power motor that drove the thirty-six inch wheels via helical gears; braking was electro-pneumatic, the retardation control operating the two blocks on each wheel: there was a service retardation of 2.25 m.p.h. per second normal, three miles per hour per second emergency. And the designed maximum speed given sixty percent full field was sixty miles per hour. The impact would be perfectly adequate to detonate and the braking couldn't help but be much too late. So it was all going to happen, and happen for what purpose? These people could have got their way with far less slaughter, it was a senseless killing: yet there was a certain logic. When they blew the system, when they flooded it, they would make a point in the biggest possible way. The world would be well able to assess the cost of attempting to frustrate terrorism: and the threat was so big that it might yet never have to be put into operation. Shard's head whirled: but he forced himself to realise that it was a bigger thing than the mere weighing of two much-wanted terrorists against a city and its population. In a very real sense, the future of any viable government was now at stake. Whatever the factors in the balance might be, the basic truth remained even clearer than ever: it didn't pay to give in to terrorism. Which was what the Prime Minister would have in mind.

*   *   *

'Hesseltine. Yes?'

'This is the Prime Minister. Have you any further—'

'I was about to ring you, sir. The woman's

just contacted again. She won't talk, she sticks to her demands. It's a simple yes or no.'

'Is there any indication of the *site* of the threat?'

'None, sir. I tried ... but I didn't expect much. She wouldn't be giving that away.'

'You've spoken to her. Do you think she can be fooled?'

Hesseltine asked, 'In what way, sir?'

'*Apparent* agreement.'

'No, sir.' Hesseltine, well into the eleventh hour, sweated blood. 'The moment anything goes wrong, she blows. I'm sure about that, quite sure. That's much too dangerous. It has to be clean—one or the other, a straight decision.' He waited, tensely, with no more to offer.

'I suppose you've no word of Shard?'

'No, sir.'

'Any theories?'

'He could have been taken, sir. We've nothing to go on.'

There was a longish silence on the line from Downing Street. Then the Prime Minister, speaking heavily, wearily, said, 'I'm handling this in the only way that seems left, Hesseltine. Tell the Commissioner, I'm ordering the two men to be given safe conduct to the Maracaibo flight. After that, it's up to Washington—but I'll be stressing to the President personally, we have one of our top men in their hands—'

'And still London, sir! This threat lasts till the men reach Maracaibo safely.'

'I know. But this is all that can be done. Except one more thing. I'm contacting London Transport personally. I want all power cut to the underground lines as soon as the men are aboard the TWA flight. Then a full-scale search by the army. These people are somewhere in the system. They have to be found.'

*   *   *

It was a compromise, and it was probably doomed to failure: but it was all that could be done. On that point there was agreement at the Yard. With the underground shut down, a large number of lives would be saved, though more troops would die if the explosion should still come. It just might not: there was good reasoning behind the Prime Minister's decision. With the wanted men in flight, clear of Britain's authority, the game would be considered at least half won: the shutting off of power might leave the terrorists merely undecided, unwilling to jeopardise the operation of getting their men safely landed in Venezuela, to play the trump card too soon. They might not precipitate.

At least it was a chance.

To Shard it came as victory for terrorism: the telephone from the man, the ally in sewage control, gave the word, received by the Arab spokesman in the power house.

'We have a go.'

A broad smile split the dark face as the Arab replaced the telephone. He passed the glad news to Shard, whose face remained impassive, not registering the tumbling, varied thoughts and reactions. Hedge appeared to be offering up a thanksgiving: Shard didn't feel quite like joining him, disliking the sour taste of professional defeat. And also not yet seeing salvation: they were not yet free. He looked back at his gaoler.

'Happy?'

'Very happy, Mr Shard. And your government has been most sensible.'

'And us? My chief and I?'

'You remain—for now, at least.'

'Hostages still?'

The man nodded, caressing the gun. 'Hostages, yes, in case your government, or the American president, should cease being sensible.'

'You think that's likely, do you?'

'Who can say? We have only overcome the start, so far. There is much to go, much distance to Maracaibo, Mr Shard.'

'Sure.' Shard looked at him sardonically. 'You think the Americans might be ... difficult?'

'It is possible. But not likely, perhaps. You and America are still largely the same people.

275

They would not, I think, be much worried about you and your Hedge, but for London, yes, for London they will have a regard.'

'In other words, the threat's still on?' As the Arab confirmed this, Shard looked again at Hedge and saw the result of prayer unanswered, of thanksgiving thrown cruelly back in his face. Hedge looked paralysed with hope cast down. In Shard's mind was the thankful thought that Beth would be all right now: she usually kept her visits to her aunt as brief as possible, and Maracaibo was a good few flying hours away. But now Beth was going to have anxiety to contend with: this thing could hardly remain out of the public eye for much longer. It was on the cards that it would be blown on the next news broadcast, and then Beth would guess, and again face the facts of being a policeman's wife.

The telephone went again: the Arab answered, smiled, rang off and looked at Shard. 'We have lift-off,' he said. 'The aircraft has left Heathrow.'

Below the open end of the dug-out connexion shaft, another train rattled through towards Waterloo. After the echoes had died away, there was silence, a silence that lasted. For a while no one ticked over: Shard in fact was the first to do so. Too long an interval between trains: somewhere, somebody was moving in positive action. He watched the faces of the men with the guns, saw, at last, the dawning puzzlement, the beginnings of anxiety and doubt.

'They have stopped the trains!'

'Correct,' Shard said. 'Now, I wonder why! And I wonder if it's the whole system . . . or just this section?'

'Just this section . . .' The dark eyes flashed. 'What good will it do, to close in on us, if that is your suggestion?' The man pointed down the shaft. 'We still have the upper hand, Mr Shard. Your people cannot doubt the facts: as soon as there is trouble, the explosion will come.'

'It will—will it? Without a train to act as your detonator?'

'The drop alone will be enough.'

'A mere twelve feet?'

The Arab smiled. 'We can't be certain. Neither can you. Which of us is going to back his belief?'

'Don't look at me,' Shard said. The gunman could be right. Possibly there would be little actual difference in impact.

★   ★   ★

Time passed: the gentlemen from the Middle East, Shard fancied, were growing edgy. They didn't like the silence: they were imagining all kinds of things creeping up on them. Maybe, now their men were airborne, they were thinking more in terms of living on to enjoy the

277

fruits of victory, the gratitude of their mates on the shores of the Eastern Mediterranean, or the Red Sea, or the Persian Gulf ... when the heady imminence of glorious death receded, the mind could become a shade less euphoric. Shard, not losing sight of the fact that the threat still remained, felt a small shift in his direction. He tried to make a dispassionate assessment of the situation in the world above: the flight to Maracaibo might well be shadowed, either by the British or by the Americans. It would certainly be causing intense diplomatic activity in the capitals and along the transatlantic telephone cables: but what, in fact, could be done? If it was an acceptable risk to jeopardise the lives of the crew, the pilot could be given his orders to deviate to a U.S. airfield: the main risk was still only London's. Much would depend on the assessment made by the President in person; his advisers might suggest a degree of bluff on the part of the subterranean gunmen. That could be an appealing argument, and one made more convincing by five thousand miles of water ...

Shard looked at his watch: seven ten. The aircraft would be well out over the Atlantic now, flying high, carrying the lives of millions beyond its own confines. At supersonic speeds ... there was time yet, but none to lose. In order to give the White House a free hand, the load of plutonium had to be rendered safe:

278

Shard's heart contracted at the huge implications of an easy statement. Across the compartment, sitting with his back against the wall, Hedge stared vacantly into space.

CHAPTER TWENTY

Suddenly, devastatingly, Hedge screamed.

Shard snapped, 'Shut up!'

It went on, high, penetrating, horrible. The boss Arab lifted his gun, fired it, sending a bullet into the plastic seat of the bench. Hedge stopped with his mouth wide open, then started choking. Shard reached out and bashed away at his back. The choking eased. Hedge was weeping now, and trembling all over. He waved his arms and gabbled indistinctly, then tried more slowly.

'I'm not the one you want. I'm not the Head of Security. You made a mistake. I'm only a screen, a front man ... *a hedge*, don't you see? Hedge isn't my name, it's a function. I'm not really important.' He was pleading, abject, his background failing to sustain him at last. 'Please, won't you let me go?'

The Arab's face was murderous. Reaching out, he gave Hedge two stinging back-handers across the cheeks: they left heavy weals. Hedge cringed. The Arab used a descriptive four-letter word, and spat. Thick saliva drooled down the face of Hedge, but he hardly seemed to notice. He pleaded again. 'Will you let me go? I'll do anything . . . anything you ask.'

The answer was another back-hander and a throaty growl: 'I will not let you go. You are of some importance—you will have to pray to your God that you are of enough importance!'

Hedge put his head in his hands and sobbed. Shard felt icy cold, not with contempt for he could understand the effect of terror on any man; but with alarm for the future: Hedge, stupid terrified Hedge, had now effectively blown his cover. If ever they happened to come out of this, four terrorists were going to know the truth, and even from gaol would spread it. Hedge would wither, though at the moment he obviously didn't care about his job. The Arab shouted at him: 'Sit down or I will shoot. You will not die, but you will be in pain.'

Hedge didn't seem to hear. He had begun screaming again, his face all crumpled like a baby's. Shard, risking a bullet himself, scrambled to his feet and made towards Hedge, and Hedge, with a terrible result, side-stepped. he side-stepped into the hole in the floor, and went down fast, carried by his own weight. As he went the side of his head struck the lip of the hole, hard. His body vanished into the shaft: the rope securing the cases of plutonium to the ring-bolt in the wall jerked bar-taut and started trembling: up top there was panic. Three of the Arabs rushed headlong for the door, were stopped by the boss man's gun. Shard shouted at them to help: shaking like leaves, they hauled the rope with him, looking surprised to be still alive. There was weight on the rope, a good sign: slowly Hedge reappeared, inch by inch of him coming up atop the bomb-cases, virtually a human nuclear bomb himself, blood pouring from his head. He had been dead lucky: he was unconscious but had dropped neatly, with his crutch smack onto one of the containers, his legs astride and his body presumably held in place, upright, by the shaft walls themselves. If he had been conscious, the crutch-landing would have hurt like hell. Shard himself got a grip on Hedge, then drew him clear of the shaft. His next action was immediate, giving no time for anticipation: with all his strength he hurled the deadweight of Hedge at the clustered, rope-holding Arabs. They yelled, falling in a heap as Hedge struck home: down the shaft again went the cases, falling fast. Shard waited for the end of the world, but the rope held. By this time he had followed up the advantage gained by the impact of Hedge, had put one of the Arabs flat on his back with his fist, and had grabbed the man's gun as it fell, flinging himself to the ground as the other opened up. Rolling over and over he fetched up by the door, fired back from the ground, taking

281

one of the terrorists right between the eyes. The head seemed to open up, and the man fell on the spot, pouring blood. As Shard scrambled up a bullet took him in the flesh of his upper arm, and he spun with the impact of a heavy calibre revolver, spun away from the doorway to reel against the wall outside. The Arabs crowded out: in the walkway outside above the main sewer Shard was in darkness, beyond the glow from the power house. He took aim, fired again. There was a brief scream, and a body flopped into the sewer stream. Shard heard running footsteps along the walkway, then rapid splashing—men going the other way. Then an apparition appeared in the doorway, staggering and falling about: Hedge, back to life.

Shard called to him: 'Hedge. Hold it! I'm going after the two that are left. Stay where you are.'

Hedge didn't seem to hear. He lurched forward from the doorway and Shard wasn't quite fast enough. On the edge of the walkway Hedge's unsteady feet slipped away and he fell, hit his head, and splashed into the stream. There was a gurgle as London sewage slimed its way into Hedge's mouth. Desperately in the light from the doorway Shard looked, straining his eyes: no Hedge, who had slid away as it were on the tide, headed for God knew where in the total dark.

Shard felt sick: but he had a job to finish and he went on to do it.

★   ★   ★

The patrol car stank and the cause was fifty percent Shard. Using the police radio he called the Yard: 'Mr Hesseltine or the Commissioner, most urgent. This is Shard.'

No delay: 'Shard, for Christ's sake—'

'Hold it and listen. The threat's over. Tell the Prime Minister immediately, as far as London's concerned, the aircraft can be deviated. The army's dealing with the explosive.'

'And Hedge?'

'Pongs a bit, but safe. I found him on the way back ... climbing out of a sewer. He wasn't really in much danger—it's not all that deep. I'll explain later. In the meantime I think I'm going to be sick. Over and out.' Shard flopped in the car seat, virtually collapsing. Through half-closed eyes he gazed at Hedge, who was looking agonised and was still holding his crutch—and who was covered in slimy un-nameables, the other fifty percent of the stench. He said in a hard voice, 'It's all right, Hedge. Those Arabs won't talk now. You blew and I covered. You're okay. And I'll keep mum—being loyalty personified! Think yourself bloody lucky!'

'You mean—?'

'I mean,' Shard said, 'I caught them and I killed them. In your interest, Hedge. And in something else you hold dear when you're safe in the Foreign Office: the *national* interest.'

Cleaned up, filled with hot soup and some neat Scotch, Shard lost no time in reporting personally to the Head of Security. 'When I'd finished in the sewer . . . I went down the shaft they'd dug. I dropped—I knew the current was off—'

'You *knew*?'

'Guessed,' Shard said briefly, still feeling the horror of not being sure. 'There seemed a certain degree of urgency. Along the tunnel, I met a stopped train and the army advancing through it. I sent them to bring Hedge down, with a rope ladder.'

'A long drop,' the chief murmured. 'For you, I mean.'

'I'm a fit man, basically. I'll be fitter when I've been home for some sleep. I—' he broke off as one of the chief's telephones burred softly. The chief answered, nodded, rang off, a mixture of emotions flickering across his face.

'The Prime Minister, Shard. The TWA flight crashed into the sea off Nassau, trying to make Windsor Field.' He sent a long breath whistling through his teeth. 'Death, I suppose, was better than a life sentence in America. Well, we're well rid of them.'

284

'But they took the flight crew with them?'

The chief nodded. 'I'm afraid so. Heroes . . . or does that sound—'

'It sounds right, sir. I'm bloody sorry. There are others too.'

'Police—I know.' The chief's tone was sombre. He flicked ash from a cigarette and went on more briskly. 'Bad as it is, Shard, there's a bright side: terrorism has been taught a lesson. It doesn't help them, when their own top men end up dead. Next time, they'll think twice. The P.M.'s grateful to you and Hedge. So is the President. And so am I.'

'Thank you, sir,' Shard said, conscious of feeling bloody-minded about Hedge. 'It's not quite over yet, though, is it?'

'As near as makes no difference—'

'But the woman?'

'I was coming to that. She's in custody—'

'Great! How, sir?'

'Hesseltine's been on the line. They picked her up in a car beating it out of London on the A23 . . . a patrolling mobile, wonderfully wide awake. Plus two men answering the description of your friends from Stalling Busk—'

'Terry and Nigel?'

'Could be. As yet, no names. That'll come! They won't be kid-gloved, Shard.'

'I'm glad to hear it!' Shard rubbed at his eyes. 'There's still a bunch of sewermen.'

'Not your worry for now. You won't be fit for

anything till you've had some sleep.'

It was Shard's worry all right, but he wasn't going to argue the point for the moment. There were enough coppers to cope. He was driven home to Ealing, thinking thoughts of Tom Casey and the DC from York, and sundry London policemen, not to mention the skewered body that had gone into the Buttertubs up in the Pennine fells. When he got home, Mrs Micklam was still in residence and had a good deal to say. They'd had a wretched day because of his rudeness and Beth had been worried—as she'd confessed when a power cut on the underground had sent them home on a bus—by something he'd said. Power cuts or not, he had no right to upset people, Mrs Micklam maintained. Shard let the voice rattle on till it was brought up short by a news flash. He poured himself a whisky and, with his back to Mrs Micklam, caught Beth's eye.

*   *   *

Next morning Hedge was back to form, hedging fast but moving stiffly. He sent for Shard and, as fully expected, put across a line with a world of meaning behind it. He said in a withdrawn voice, 'I've received congratulations from a number of quite prominent people. There's talk of honours.' He coughed, glancing sideways at Shard. 'I don't know that I deserve

286

it, of course—'

'No.'

Hedge bridled at that. 'I don't much like your tone. Was that an . . . *interrogative* no?'

'No.'

'Please don't be impertinent, Shard. I was going on to say . . . what I did was not much . . . but I thought a diversion would be of help to you. I fancy it was. If it hadn't been for me, you wouldn't have had your chance. I know you'll see that—h'm?'

Shard laughed in his face. 'Don't bother to press, I won't say a thing. Except that you're as big a bastard as ever, Hedge. And that's safe with me, too.'

'I'm sorry you feel that way, Shard,' Hedge said, stiffer than ever. 'I simply did what I could. If you remember—I didn't want to go in the first place.' He dismissed Shard after that, and Shard went back to Seddon's Way simmering. Honours! Sir Hedge, Lord Hedge, or just Hedge CBE? Five days later a little temporary poetic justice came along: Hedge was sick. There was a high fever, with rigours, headache, vomiting, severe muscular pain, plus facial congestion, infected conjunctivae and a labial herpes. Hedge had gone from pink to orange and had a stiff neck: it all sounded very nasty and it added up to Weil's Disease: Hedge wouldn't be back inside a month.